THE SCHOOL THAT'S OUT OF THIS WORLD

Hyperspace High is first published in the United States by
Stone Arch Books
A Capstone imprint
1710 Roe Crest Drive
North Mankato, Minnesota 56003
www.capstonepub.com

First published in 2013 by Curious Fox
an imprint of Capstone Global Library Limited,
7 Pilgrim Street, London, EC4V 6LB
Registered company number: 6695582
www.curious-fox.com

Text © Hothouse Fiction Ltd 2013
Series created by Hothouse Fiction
www.hothousefiction.com
The author's moral rights are hereby asserted.

Library of Congress Cataloging-in-Publication Data is available on the
Library of Congress website.
ISBN: 978-1-4342-6568-5 (library binding)
ISBN: 978-1-4342-7935-4 (paperback)

Summary: It's the end of the semester, and the students are in the grip of
revision fever…until a real fever takes over. The only possible cure lies in
a distant nebula, but with the whole school under quarantine, who will be
brave enough to go and get it?

Designer: Alison Thiele

With special thanks to Martin Howard

Printed in China.
092013   007749WAIMANS14

SPACE PLAGUE

written by ZAC HARRISON • illustrated by DANI GEREMIA

▼▼ STONE ARCH BOOKS™
a capstone imprint www.capstonepub.com

CHAPTER 1

A fat, black, octopus-like creature with red eyes and a drooling slit of a mouth tapped a tentacle on the desk impatiently. "Well, John Riley, do you know the answer or not?" it asked him, slobbering.

John ran a hand through his messy mop of blond hair, his forehead lined in concentration. He leaned forward in his MorphSeat and glanced around the bright classroom, desperately looking for a clue to the answer.

In the seat next to him, a beautiful silver-haired girl from the planet Sillar lifted her shoulders in a shrug. Emmie Tarz didn't know the answer, either.

"Umm . . . yes, Doctor Graal," John said eventually. "The soil structure on planet Bezkel is unusual because . . . uhhh . . ."

"Please stop mumbling and state the answer clearly, so the whole class can hear," said the Gargon teacher.

Blushing, John stammered an answer: "It's unusual b-because there's — you know — alien stuff in it . . ."

Doctor Graal glared at him. "That will do, Mister Riley. It is quite obvious that you do not know the answer. It worries me to think how you will do with your exams. If, by some miracle, you pass, I suggest you pay more attention next semester." Turning away, she continued,

"Who can tell me what is unusual about the soil structure on planet Bezkel . . . oh, of course. Mordant Talliver."

A few seats along from John, the half-Gargon boy with black hair lowered one of the two long, black tentacles that sprouted from his ribcage. "Every century Bezkel has a ten-year solar eclipse," he answered quickly. "Most plant life dies, producing layers of extremely rich, dark soil. This creates an especially plentiful growing season once the eclipse has passed."

"Excellent answer, Mordant," blubbered the teacher. "I'm so glad someone has been paying attention."

Mordant shot a sly glance at John. "Learning must be difficult when your brain isn't fully evolved," he whispered, loud enough for John to hear.

Lights flickered across the surface of a small

silver sphere that floated at Mordant's shoulder. "How witty you are, young Master Talliver. And how right. The Earthling does not deserve to be in the same classroom as you," droned his constant companion, the Serve-U-Droid, G-Vez.

"Yeah, primitive life forms belong in zoos," Mordant muttered, sniggering.

Furious, John opened his mouth to retort. A hand gripped his shoulder. Turning around quickly, he saw his friend Kaal shake his head. A native of the planet Derril, Kaal's green skin, sharp fangs, and leathery wings made him look like a demon. In his case, though, looks were deceiving: Kaal was a shy, clever student and a good friend. As John watched, the Derrilian put a finger to his lips.

Blushing an even deeper red, John ground his teeth together. Kaal was right. Getting into a fight with Mordant Talliver, especially in Doctor Graal's Galactic Geography class, was asking for trouble. The half-Gargon boy was the teacher's favorite, and she was sure to take his side. As Mordant knew well, John would land himself a detention, or worse, if he took the bait. Biting back a retort, John turned back to face Doctor Graal instead, muttering, "Maybe I'd pay more attention in class if you ever said anything interesting," under his breath.

Fortunately, the Gargon teacher didn't hear. She had lifted a metal box onto the desk with her tentacles and was busy unfastening the clips that secured its lid. "I have a very exciting sample here," she said. "An important rock formation from the planet Zhaldaria that I found in a storage chamber at the Pan-Galactic Geography Institute during the last school holiday. It hasn't been opened for a very long time, but if the label is correct, it should be a perfect example of how a planet's changing weather systems affect its soil structure."

Yay, more soil. Too much excitement, thought John. As he leaned back in his MorphSeat, it adjusted around his new position. Hearing a sigh from the next desk, he glanced around. Emmie rolled her navy blue eyes. John winked at her, knowing that his friend was thinking exactly the same thing. Both of them hated Galactic Geography lessons.

At the front of the class, Doctor Graal's eyes lit up as the lid of the box flipped open. "Oh, yes," she said, drooling over the soil, "it's a fine example. How absolutely wonderful." Two tentacles dipped into the box and pulled out a rock the size of a soccer ball. Wobbling forward, she slithered from one desk to the next, showing her exhibit to the students. "Zhaldarian rock is fascinating to study because in ancient times the planet's weather system changed so frequently," she said. "Note the different-colored bands. Each layer was, at one point in history, the surface of Zhaldaria. By analyzing the bands, galactic geologists can tell exactly what happened in the planet's ecosystem over many thousands of years. It is especially rare because Zhaldaria's star — Zaleta — went supernova almost a million years ago, forming the Zaleta Nebula. This small piece of rock is probably all that is left of a once thriving planet."

John leaned forward, trying his best to look interested, as Doctor Graal turned the lump of rock this way and that in front of him. As she moved on, he shrugged.

Yeah, fascinating, he thought.

"What does this band tell us about Zhaldaria's weather?" asked Kaal once Doctor

Graal reached his desk, running a finger along a ribbon of black that ran through the center of the rock.

"Students must not touch," snapped the teacher, slapping Kaal's hand away with one of her tentacles. "This sample is extremely old and delicate. To answer your question, the black band dates from the first appearance of Zhaldarian Flu, which wiped out the entire Zhaldarian race before spreading across the universe."

"Yuck," said Kaal, wiping his hand on his silver and red jumpsuit uniform.

Doctor Graal rolled her eyes. "There is no danger. There hasn't been a single case of Zhaldarian Flu in over two hundred years," she said.

A bell sounded, ending the class. Around the classroom, students chattered while they slipped their portable ThinScreen computers into carry cases.

Gently placing her rock back in its box, Doctor Graal shouted over the noise. "Class dismissed, but don't forget — final exams begin tomorrow. I expect you all to study constantly until then, especially Emmie Tarz and John Riley. If you fail, you will not be returning to Hyperspace High next semester."

"I'll send G-Vez to help you both with your packing if you like," Mordant quipped. "You might as well get started right away."

Emmie's blue eyes glinted dangerously as she turned on the half-Gargon. "Why don't you do that," she hissed. "It will give me a chance to throw your nasty little droid out of an airlock."

"Oh I say, Master Talliver. Are you going to let her —"

"Do you always have to be such a jerk,

Mordant?" John cut in, his hands balling into fists.

A grin spread across Mordant Talliver's face.

"Is there a problem, Mordant?" Doctor Graal called over.

"John just called me a —"

"There's no problem, Doctor Graal," Kaal said, interrupting the exchange with a forced laugh. "We're just joking around." Taking John's shoulder with one enormous hand and Emmie's with the other, he pushed them both through the door and into the hallway outside. "John and Emmie were just saying they're on their way to study right now," he bellowed over his shoulder, drowning out Mordant's indignant protests as he steered his friends through the crowd of students leaving the classroom.

Once they'd bumped and jostled their way out of Doctor Graal's earshot, the Derrilian crossed his arms and sighed. "That was stupid," he said. "You know Mordant's trying to get you in trouble before exams."

"I know," said John. "I can't help it. He's such a —"

"Spiteful, smug, arrogant waste of atoms," Emmie remarked, finishing the sentence for him. She hooked a strand of long silvery hair behind one of her pointed ears and scowled. "What's his problem anyway? Does he wake up every morning and think 'I'm going to be a nasty, obnoxious bully today'?"

Kaal passed a hand across his face — the Derrilian equivalent of a shrug, John had learned — then patted Emmie on the shoulder. "Gargons," he said, "you know what they're like. Can't you just ignore him?"

"Psh," Emmie said, snorting. "I haven't forgotten what he did during the Space

15

Spectacular. He tried to wreck my friendship with you guys."

"It would be great if we could ignore him," said John, "but he's really good at getting under our skin. He knows Emmie and I are worried about failing the exams, and with me only being here by accident . . ."

John's voice trailed off. As both of his friends knew, he was worried that he didn't really belong at Hyperspace High. The school, housed on an enormous spaceship, was the best in the universe, and all of its students were specially selected. All except John, that is. Eight weeks earlier he had been mistaken for a Martian prince and accidentally whisked away from Earth. Since then, Headmaster Lorem had given John a permanent place and told him many times that he belonged here as much as any of the other students.

Even so, John still had a nagging feeling that Mordant was right: he didn't deserve his place at Hyperspace High.

"Don't let Mordant get to you," said Kaal seriously. "He's an idiot, and the last thing you need right now is trouble. Try to stay out of his way for the next few days."

"That sounds like a great plan to me," John said. "The less I see of him, the better."

"Same here," said Emmie. "Anyway, come on, John — we should get going."

"Aren't you coming to the Center with me?" Kaal asked, frowning. "You know I hate eating by myself."

John punched his arm. "Somehow you'll just have to survive without us," he said with a grin. "I hate to say this, but for once Doctor Graal's right. Emmie and I have to study, or neither of us stands a chance."

"We'll be in the library if you want us," Emmie added. "Come on, John."

"Wait up, you guys!" Kaal called to Bareon and Lishtig, who were heading to the Center. John and Emmie padded down the thickly carpeted hall in the opposite direction, toward a TravelTube.

* * *

"Library," the TravelTube announced as its door opened with a quiet *vipp*.

The first time John had visited the school library, he had expected it to be bigger. However, there was no need for a large library on a spaceship where every student could access all the information held in its massive data banks from anywhere on board. Most students preferred to study in their own dorm rooms, and some didn't even realize there was a library on board. Only students who had noisy roommates or who just liked the place used it. John was one of the latter. The shelves of ancient books reminded him of libraries on Earth, though the precious books here were protected behind glass. Beautiful holo-paintings hung from the walls, while soft lamps gave the room a cozy atmosphere.

"What's on the study schedule for tonight, Zepp?" Emmie asked the ship's computer, as she dropped her bag on a desk in the middle of the empty room and sat in a MorphSeat that immediately adjusted to fit her perfectly.

From nowhere a friendly voice answered. "You will be delighted to learn that tonight is the night to study Galactic Geography."

John had named the ship's computer Zepp — short for Zero-Electronic Personality

Program — soon after arriving at the school. Since then, everyone in the school had started using the name.

Groaning, John pulled a second MorphSeat over and sat beside Emmie. "We just had Galactic Geography," he said, complaining. "You're trying to torture us, aren't you, Zepp?"

"Torturing is prohibited by my programming," the computer replied. "You will study more efficiently while the subject is still fresh in your minds."

The large ThinScreen on the desk in front of John and Emmie switched on.

"Let's review the classwork from the beginning of term," Zepp's voice continued. "We'll start with the general galactic mapping, cover planet formation and weather systems, and then move on to nebulae."

At once, the ThinScreen created a perfect

3-D image of a galaxy in the air between John and Emmie. Spinning slowly, a glowing spiral made up of billions of tiny stars lit up their faces.

"Okay, then," said Zepp. "Who can show me the Scutum-Centaurus Arm?"

Emmie looked blank. John reached out and touched one of the bands of light that curved out from the galactic center. It flashed blue, while the words "Scutum-Centaurus" appeared above it.

Over the next half hour, the computer quizzed the two students on the structure of the galaxy.

"Now, we need to move on," said Zepp eventually. A glittering cloud of gases, lit from within by millions of stars, blazed in the dim library. "John, can you tell me what a nebula is?"

John knew this one. "Nebulae are massive clouds of dust and gases, formed when large stars explode," he answered.

"Large stars aren't the only things exploding. I think my head is about to burst," muttered Emmie.

"Try to pay attention," Zepp said smoothly. "Inside the nebula's core, the gravity is constant while the temperature reaches up to . . ." As the computer went into detail about each type of nebula, John's hand ached from scribbling notes with the stylus onto his ThinScreen.

Finally, Emmie hopped out of her seat. With a wave of her hand, she scattered the holographic nebula into pixels that floated around the room. "Enough," she said. "I'm not kidding. Any more of this and my brain is going to start dribbling out of my ears. Plus, we probably won't even need to know half that stuff."

"You might be right," said Zepp's voice. "You probably should take a break. No one ever passed an exam with their brain dribbling out of their ears."

"Those are the wisest words I've heard all day," Emmie said, sighing. Reaching down, she grabbed John's hand and pulled him upright. "Come on, Earthling. I need to blow off some steam."

CHAPTER 2

Emmie led John to one of Hyperspace High's gymnasiums, a large hemisphere that looked like the inside of a gigantic metal ball that had been chopped in half.

Running to the equipment room, she pressed her hand to a wall panel. A door slid open. Emmie walked in and emerged a few seconds later pushing a ball that was at least as tall as John.

"Uhhh, what's this for?" he asked, confused. "Are we playing mega soccer?"

"Cyber jousting," replied Emmie over her shoulder as she disappeared into the closet again. "Seriously, John? Don't tell me you've never done it before."

"Never even heard of cyber jousting!" John shouted after her.

"That means I'm going to totally kick your butt, then," Emmie said, grinning as she pushed another giant ball out of the closet. "You can help set up by placing the balls in the middle of the room about thirty feet apart while I get everything else we need."

John did as he was told, while Emmie returned to the equipment room. When she came out this time, she was carrying two pairs of shoes, what looked like large guns with long, wide muzzles, and two QuickFans — used for flying in zero gravity. "The rules of cyber jousting are simple," she said. "You balance on the ball and fire your gun at your opponent to knock them off."

"Sounds easy enough."

Emmie grinned again as she pulled on the special shoes and clipped a QuickFan to her belt. "You'll soon find out it's harder than it sounds," she said. "Trust me. The gun shoots small balls and, because there's no gravity, they'll be constantly bouncing off the walls. The gun only has ten balls. To reload, you'll have to catch others as they fly past. Fall off and your opponent wins a point. First person to ten wins the match."

"What are the shoes for?" John asked as he slipped his foot into one. He noticed that the sole was metallic.

"Since we're playing in zero-g, the slightest movement will send you flying all over the hall," Emmie told him. "The shoes are lightly magnetized to help keep your feet on the ball, but it's still really, really easy to fall off. If you do fall off, use the QuickFan to get back on the ball again. Ready?"

"Ready," said John, standing up and shouldering his gun. "All right, Tarz. Prepare to taste defeat."

Emmie flicked back her long, silvery hair and pulled it into a ponytail. "Oh, I don't think so," she said, smiling. Speaking more loudly, she added, "All right, Zepp — put us into zero gravity now, please."

"Certainly, Emmie," said Zepp's voice. "Be gentle with him, won't you?"

"Probably not," Emmie replied, smirking as the computer turned off the gravity. With one elegant bound, she jumped to the top of one of the large balls, finding her balance instantly. With her feet, she expertly rolled the ball in a small circle until she faced John.

"Come on, Earthling, what are you waiting for?"

Copying Emmie's move, John leaped for the top of the other ball. As his feet touched down, the ball began rolling away.

"Aaah!" he yelled, arms flailing as he tumbled straight off again, floating away across the sports hall.

"I'm still preparing myself to taste defeat," Emmie said. She giggled as John flicked on his

QuickFan, using the tiny jet to propel him back toward the ball.

On the third attempt, John finally managed to balance. Swaying, he tried aiming his gun. With the ball shifting beneath his feet, the muzzle swung about wildly.

"Okay!" shouted Emmie. "Joust in three . . . two . . . one . . . go."

"Oooof!" John grunted as he was thrown from the ball.

Emmie's first shot had hit him squarely in the chest.

"One point to me!" Emmie yelled, punching the air. "Get back on the ball, Earthling."

Twice more, Emmie managed to shoot John off his ball before he'd had a chance to even pull the trigger.

As he took position for the third time, he

gritted his teeth, thinking, *Come on, John. You are being humiliated.*

Concentrating, he brought his gun up and, at last, squeezed off a shot. The ball went wide. Whistling past Emmie, it bounced against the wall and came hurtling back.

"Nooo!" John yelped, trying to roll out of the way. He was too slow. The ball smacked him in the center of his forehead, sending him spinning across the sports hall once more.

Emmie was laughing hysterically as John mounted the ball again. "That was incredible," she said, "Zepp, did you record that? Please say yes. I'm going to have to show it to everyone I know." With tears of laughter streaming from her eyes, the muzzle of her gun weaved about unsteadily.

A ball whistled through the air toward John. Jerking his shoulder, he managed to get out of the way just in time. He pulled the trigger on his gun.

Emmie's laughter ended abruptly, as John's shot hit her on the thigh, sending her tumbling.

"Hey!" she cried. "That's not supposed to happen."

"I think I'm starting to get the hang of it now," John replied smoothly.

"Well, I was taking it easy on you," she said, grinning. Emmie leaped back onto her ball. "But if you think you're ready to play for real . . ." A shot zoomed across the sports hall.

Wobbling, John ducked. He aimed his gun and almost brought Emmie down again with a ball that glanced off her ankle. It joined the others, which were now zipping around the room.

"I'll get you for that!"

Before John knew it, he was flying backward

again. With a blast of the QuickFan, he was back on the ball, now finding his balance more easily. "Five-one!" he shouted. "You haven't won yet, Emmie!"

Over the next half hour, they played three matches. Emmie won the first two easily, but John learned fast. The last match was hard-fought, and the Sillaran girl only just scraped a ten-nine victory.

"Not bad," she said, leaping gracefully to the floor, as Zepp restored gravity. "In another few years, you might make a half-decent cyber jouster."

"Ha, you were lucky in that last match," John told her, wiping sweat from his forehead. "If that rebound hadn't hit me from behind, I would have wiped the floor with you."

"You think?"

"Definitely."

"Quick rematch?" said Emmie, raising an eyebrow.

"I'm sorry to interrupt," said Zepp's voice, "but this sports hall is reserved for a Plutonian Karate tournament in five minutes. I would also recommend rest if you wish to be fresh for your exams in the morning."

Already, the sports hall was turning into a karate arena around them. The floor beneath their feet transformed into a spongy mat. Bleachers slid out from the walls.

"Another time, then," said John with a mock growl. "But don't think I'm going to forget I owe you a trouncing."

"We'll see about that, Earthling," Emmie said with a smile.

By the time the two of them had returned their equipment to the equipment room, students began arriving for the tournament.

Rosy-cheeked and still chuckling, John and Emmie set off for the TravelTube at the end of the corridor.

"You were getting pretty good toward the end," Emmie said.

"Not as good as you," John replied. "But it's a fun game. Where does it come from?"

"It wasn't a game when it started," his friend told him. "Cyber jousting began as a fight to the death between specially trained warriors. Matches were fought in space, and only the winner came back. Anyone who lost contact with their ball was left to drift off between the stars, never to be seen again."

"We're going to stick to the gym, though, right?" John asked, shivering.

A few weeks earlier, he and Kaal had almost died in the cold vacuum of space during the Robot Warriors' competition — and the memory still chilled him.

The door of the TravelTube opened in front of them. "Luckily for you," Emmie replied, "cyber jousting in space is now illegal."

"Dormitory level sixteen," said the TravelTube, as its door slid open a few seconds later.

John and Emmie stepped out into a wide common room that looked like a hotel lobby. Soft sofas were scattered across the heavily carpeted floor. A small fountain bubbled in the middle of the room. Lining the walls were plasma sculptures created by former Hyperspace High students who had gone on to become famous artists.

Realizing just how tired he was, John said goodnight to Emmie and then crossed the floor to his own room. As the door slid open, he stumbled into the dimly lit room. Then he stopped.

Something was different.

John looked around, slightly confused. The two black sofas were exactly where they should be. So, too, were the desks he and Kaal worked at. On the other side of the floor-to-ceiling window, stars slipped by as the huge school made its way through the skies.

What's different? John thought.

A moment later, he realized. At this time of the day, Kaal was usually sitting on one of the sofas, either playing on the virtual-reality games console they had won in the Robot Warriors' competition, tinkering with a piece of technology, or watching something on the entertainment ThinScreen. Since the Derrilian only needed an hour or so of sleep each night, he was almost always up studying or playing games in their room. But tonight, the room was empty.

John shrugged. *Maybe he's hanging out at Ska's Café, or went to the 4-D theater for a late showing. I'd look for him, but I'm too tired.*

Yawning, he crossed to the bathroom, climbing out of his jumpsuit and throwing it over the back of a sofa. He grabbed his toothbrush from the bathroom and flicked the entertainment ThinScreen on to the Intergalactic News Channel. A small gang of space pirates had been rounded up in the Omega Sector. Councillor Tarz — Emmie's father — had made a speech welcoming a new world to the League of Planets.

John looked with interest at the footage of Emmie's father, a tall, golden-skinned man with silvery blue hair.

Suddenly, the image changed and John heard the word "Earth," which startled him. A NASA launch had taken off, almost colliding with a cloaked intergalactic tourist cruiser in orbit. Grinning, the news reporter said that the cruiser's captain had used force fields to change the Earth rocket's direction, leaving human scientists mystified.

John thought this must be the funny story that normally took place at the end of the news. Next on was a discussion about the rising price of mallux. Boring. He flicked off the screen.

A faint rustling sound came from Kaal's bed pod. John took the toothbrush out of his mouth and peered into the small room that was completely filled by a bed.

Kaal was fast asleep.

John frowned. It was hours earlier than his roommate's usual bedtime and, normally, when

Kaal went to bed, he closed the screen in case his loud snoring bothered John.

Tonight, though, the screen had been left open.

Beneath the covers Kaal shifted slightly, his wings rustling again. There was no hint of his usual bed-shaking snores.

He completely passed out, John thought. *Must be exhausted from studying.*

Squinting in the dim light, he stepped closer, unable to believe his eyes. Kaal's skin was glowing — a luminescent green that seemed to pulse gently. Over the past few weeks at Hyperspace High, John had seen many bizarre things, but this was something new.

"Hey, Kaal," he whispered, "you're sort of glowing. Are you okay?"

Kaal slept on.

"Hello?"

There was still no response from the sleeping Derrilian.

"Maybe you just ate something fluorescent for dinner," John said quietly. "It's sort of amazing that you haven't sprouted an extra head by now with all the weird stuff you eat. Or maybe your people just glow sometimes. Honestly, it wouldn't be the freakiest thing about you guys."

Reaching out, he pressed a pad on the wall at the foot of Kaal's bed pod. The screen slid silently into place.

"Nighty night, Kaal," John called, yawning. He crossed the room to his own bed pod and climbed in.

Slipping under the covers, he laid back and stared at the ceiling with his hands behind his head. "Yup, can't wait for finals to be over," he said to himself. In a few days' time, he would board one of Hyperspace High's shuttles and return to Earth. For the first time in two months, he would see his parents in person. They had no idea that he was trillions of miles across the universe; they thought he was at a boarding school.

Oh, man, I wish I could tell everyone about Hyperspace High, he thought. *And about exploding volcano planets and alien wars and building my own robot and everything else that's happened over the last couple of months.*

John smiled as his eyes closed. *Yeah, right. Tell people at home about this place? They'd think I'd totally lost it.*

A few months ago, John would have laughed at the idea of life beyond Earth, too. But now his two best friends came from different planets —

and he couldn't imagine what he'd do without them over the holidays.

CHAPTER 3

Music filtered into John's dream — it was a song his mom often sang while dancing around the kitchen at home. He stirred, muttering, "Mom, stop it. That's sooo embarrassing."

"Morning, John," said Zepp's voice loudly. "Time to get up."

John pulled the covers up around his head. "'Nother five minutes, Mom," he mumbled.

"Two pieces of news," the computer replied. "First: I am not your mother. Second: exams start in one hour. Up and at 'em. Wakey wakey. Rise and shine."

John sat up, shaking his head. "Huh?" he mumbled. "What?"

"Exams, John. One hour. Time to get going."

"Oh great, exams," said John. "Way to make me leap out of bed with a smile on my face, Zepp."

"Cosmic Languages this morning," replied the computer. "Examination room eight. You now have fifty-seven minutes and thirty-two seconds."

John groaned. Along with Galactic Geography, Cosmic Languages was his least favorite subject. "Oh well," he said, crawling out of bed and rubbing sleep out of his eyes, "might as well get it over with."

"Shall I start the auto-cleanse for you?"

"Please, Zepp," John said, yawning. His face twisted as music started, a song called "Oh What a Beautiful Morning" from an old movie. "And turn the music off; I hate this song. My mom sings it all the time."

On John's first day at Hyperspace High, he and the computer had bonded over music. Zepp loved Earth music and played it whenever the chance arose. Some of the computer's song choices were, however, very odd.

"This is a classic," Zepp said, increasing the volume. "One of my favorite tunes. Your mother has excellent taste."

"Please, Zepp!" John shouted. "Turn it off or I'll be forced to take a large hammer to your circuits."

John sighed with relief as the song came to an abrupt stop.

"Spoilsport," said Zepp.

The auto-cleanse shower always made John feel like he was standing in a car wash. First, hundreds of tiny nozzles sprayed him all over with soap. After that the waterpower increased, filling the shower cubicle with swirling foam as the jets scoured him up and down. After a final rinse with clean water, blasts of warm air dried him off within seconds.

Fifteen minutes later, still humming, John scanned the notes he'd made on the Gularan language on his portable ThinScreen while he brushed his teeth. Rinsing his mouth, he checked the mirror to make sure his hair wasn't doing anything too weird, then wrapped a towel around himself.

Walking back into the larger room, he took a fresh silver and red Hyperspace High uniform from his locker, and started getting dressed.

"Hey, Zepp, where's Kaal?" he asked. "Did he leave for breakfast already?"

"Kaal is still in bed," said Zepp. "I've tried to wake him several times, but he just will not get up."

"That's not like him," John replied, glancing at his friend's closed bedpod screen. "Usually, he's trying to drag me to breakfast before I'm out of bed."

"It is strange. As you know, Derrilians only need one hour of sleep each day. Kaal has been in bed for almost ten hours."

Crossing the room, John placed his hand on the wall panel. The screen slid back. John blinked in surprise. During the night, Kaal had curled into a ball, his arms hugging his knees and his wings wrapped around his body. His skin was still glowing, but even brighter now. Kaal's bed pod was filled with green light.

This is freaky, John thought. Leaning over, he gently shook his friend by the shoulder. "Kaal," he said. "Wake up."

Kaal didn't move. His eyes remained closed. Beneath John's hand Kaal's skin felt hot and sticky. *Is that normal for Derrilians?* John wondered. With growing fear, he realized that he knew nothing about the way Derrilian bodies worked. Kaal might have a fever, or his species might wake up sweating fluorescent green all the time.

"Kaal," John repeated louder, shaking his roommate's shoulder again. "Stop messing around. Exams start in forty-five minutes. Get up or you're going to be late."

No response.

"KAAL!" This time, John shouted. Still, Kaal didn't move.

John leaned over further. His friend was breathing, but his breaths were fast and shallow.

This is definitely not right, John thought.

"Zepp!" John yelled, his voice cracking with concern. "I think Kaal's sick."

"Stay calm," Zepp said instantly. "I will alert the Meteor Medics. They will arrive in a few moments."

"Tell them to hurry. He looks really bad."

"They are on their way now."

"How long —"

The door hissed open, and six white robots with blue flashing lights and a flaming fireball insignia on their chests flooded into the room.

Silently, John watched as the medical droids worked on Kaal. More metal arms emerged from their robotic bodies, each dividing into dozens of smaller fingers, some carrying medical equipment that John didn't recognize. The Meteor Medics expertly turned Kaal onto his back. John winced as one of the robots began injecting probes into Kaal's glowing skin. Another Meteor Medic ran a pulsing blue light over his friend's unconscious form.

Kaal jerked. His eyes half-opened before closing again almost instantly.

"What are they doing?" John shouted, trying to get through the mass of droids. "Zepp, they're hurting him."

"John, stay calm," Zepp said sternly. "They're not hurting him. What you saw is a reaction to the Total Scan. The Meteor Medics are collecting information from every part of Kaal's body down to a cellular level. It will only take a minute."

"ANALYZING, ANALYZING . . ." droned one of the Meteor Medics in a flat, toneless voice. "RESULTS CONFIRMED."

The blue flashing lights turned red. John felt a shiver of fear run down his back.

"URGENT ACTION REQUIRED," said the robot. "QUARANTINE PATIENT. DISINFECT DORMITORY IMMEDIATELY."

"What's happening?" shouted John as another Meteor Medic hurried into the room, a floating hover stretcher close behind.

None of the droids answered him. Their spindly arms quickly lifted Kaal out of bed and onto the stretcher.

"ACTIVATE FORCE FIELD."

A glowing blue dome appeared over the stretcher.

"INFECTION CONTAINED."

The Meteor Medics began carrying the stretcher out through the door.

"Please, tell me what's happening," John yelled desperately, trying to follow. "Where are you taking him? What's wrong with Kaal?"

A Meteor Medic blocked his path, laying long metal fingers on his chest to stop him. "JOHN RILEY, HAVE YOU BEEN IN CLOSE CONTACT WITH THE PATIENT?" it asked, ignoring his questions.

"What? I don't understand what's going on here."

"HAVE YOU TOUCHED THE PATIENT?"

John tried to push the droid to one side. "I just want to see my friend!" he shouted. "Let me through."

Zepp's voice cut in. "John Riley has been in close contact with the patient," the computer confirmed. "He touched his shoulder a few moments ago."

Flashing a red light, the medic said, "JOHN RILEY, REPORT TO THE MEDICAL WING IMMEDIATELY. YOU AND YOUR

ROOMMATE HAVE BEEN EXPOSED TO
ZHALDARIAN FLU."

CHAPTER 4

Lying back on a silver examination table, wearing only his underwear, John looked up into the enormous black eyes of Dr. Kasaria, the chief of Hyperspace High's medical wing. "What is going on?" he asked. Goose bumps prickled across his skin where it touched the cold metal.

"Please be quiet and open your mouth wide,"

said the metallic-skinned woman in a curiously high voice. "I do not have time for questions."

"But —"

"Open wide."

John did as he was told. The doctor peered down his throat and then ran a small machine up and down his body. More goose bumps tingled wherever it passed.

"You're lucky. You show no sign of infection," Dr. Kasaria said briskly. "Zhaldarian Flu is extremely contagious. Report back here if you feel even a little bit sick. In the meantime, please walk through the disinfectant field, get dressed, and return to school."

"But what about Kaal?" John asked.

Dr. Kasaria's face softened. "Your friend is in good hands," she said quietly. "The ship has excellent medical facilities, and I will do everything I can for him."

"He's going to get better, though, right?"

"As I said, I will do everything I can for him," the doctor repeated. "Now, I believe you have an exam starting in ten minutes, and I must treat my patient."

John started to protest but closed his mouth. He didn't want to waste Dr. Kasaria's time when she could be taking care of Kaal.

Slipping off the examination table, he followed her pointing finger to a machine that looked like a freestanding doorframe. The machine buzzed quietly as he walked through, a pink light quickly wrapping around him and disappearing just as rapidly. A light mist hissed over his skin.

"Disinfection complete," said the voice.

John dressed in a new jumpsuit and peered into Kaal's room. Dr. Kasaria was leaning over Kaal's bed, checking the machines around him.

Knowing there was nothing else he could do, John took one last look at his friend and left the medical wing.

"John, where have you been?" Emmie cried, as John stepped out of the TravelTube. "There's only a couple of minutes until the exam . . ." Seeing the expression on John's face, she stopped. "What's the matter?"

"It's Kaal," he said. "He has Zhaldarian Flu."

Emmie stared at him, her eyes wide in shock. For a few moments, she seemed unable to speak. Her golden skin paled. "Oh no," she said, her voice quivering. "I saw the Meteor Medics disinfecting the dormitory level but just thought someone must have eaten the wrong thing . . . but this . . . this is awful." As John watched, tears formed in the corners of Emmie's eyes.

"You know about Zhaldarian Flu?" John

asked quickly. "No one's told me anything. Is Kaal in danger?"

Emmie nodded and a tear trickled down her face. "My great-great-grandmother had it when she was a girl," she answered. "For six months the doctors didn't know if she was going to live or die. There's not much the doctors can do. No cure . . . nothing."

By now, other students had noticed the tears rolling down Emmie's face. A few of Emmie and John's classmates pressed in around her, concern showing on their faces.

"Hey, Tarz. Are you okay?" asked Lishtig, a boy from the planet Slarce, whose long, purple ponytail almost reached the floor. When Emmie didn't answer, he turned to John. "What's up, John? Where's Kaal?"

"Attention, all students," a droning electronic voice announced.

Every student looked up. An Examiner was gliding along the corridor. The machine was white, with an egg-shaped body. A red light flickered across its round head as it spoke. In front of it floated a large tray. "A case of Zhaldarian Flu has been confirmed onboard Hyperspace High. Each student will wear a medical mask until further notice," the robot said.

A shocked murmur ran through the crowd of students. "But Zhaldarian Flu was eradicated centuries ago," said Raytanna, her smooth white forehead creasing in concern and her six eyes blinking.

Lishtig stared hard at John. "It's Kaal, isn't it?" he asked.

John nodded.

"What about the exams?" asked Emmie, reaching into the tray to take a mask. "Have they been canceled?"

"Negative. The case has been contained. School activities will continue as normal."

John slipped the medical mask over his face. The material immediately molded to John's skin. It felt a little like he was wearing a spiderweb.

A bell sounded. At the same time, a door slid open several feet down the corridor. A pink, snakelike alien slithered through the door. Ms. Skrinel — the Cosmic Languages teacher — always left a thin trail of slime behind her wherever she went.

"Good morning, students," she said. "The examination will start in ten minutes. Please line up quietly until your name is called. Then the Examiner will collect your personal belongings and you can make your way to your exam cube."

John's eyes widened as he walked through the door into what had been one of Hyperspace High's sports halls the day before. Now, transparent cubes had been arranged in a square around the giant room.

"John Riley."

John stepped forward. An Examiner scanned him with a beam of blue light. His pockets emptied. The ThinScreen stylus and an old watch he'd brought with him from Earth vanished. His possessions had been broken down into their individual atoms, to be reformed and returned to him at the end of the exam. The Examiners allowed nothing into the exam cubes except the students and the clothes they were wearing. As a result, no one had ever been known to cheat on a Hyperspace High exam.

"Cube twelve, John Riley," said Ms. Skrinel.

Nervously, John found his cube. As he sat in a MorphSeat, the clear door swung shut. The cube was small, but its walls quickly moved outward, allowing John more elbow room. The quiet buzz of whispering and Ms. Skrinel's voice were instantly cut off. He was alone, waiting to be examined.

As the rest of the cubes filled up with students, John breathed deeply. The events of the morning had temporarily pushed any thoughts of exams out of his mind. Now they came flooding back. If he failed, he would not be returning to Hyperspace High. He squeezed his eyes shut, trying to force his brain to focus. Memories of the morning, and of Kaal's strangely curled-up body, kept forcing their way to the front of his mind.

Cosmic Languages was not one of John's best subjects. He had never seen the point of it. The ship's systems modified sound waves so that all languages were translated into the students' native tongue. Every word John ever heard onboard Hyperspace High was in English, though no one there spoke his language. Small devices could be taken off-ship to perform the same task.

He had once asked Ms. Skrinel why anyone studied Cosmic Languages when everyone could already understand each other perfectly. Her answer had been curt, as if she had answered the same question a thousand times before: "What happens if the computer system goes down? What happens if the device breaks?"

Later, Kaal explained that Hyperspace High also taught Cosmic Languages because the students learned a lot about the universe's many species through the different ways they communicated.

That, John had decided, made much more sense. But right now, John tried to push thoughts of Kaal aside.

"Oral examination commences," said a flat

voice from nowhere. "Question one: In Derrilian, how would you say, 'I need assistance'?"

John choked. Derrilian was Kaal's native language. "I . . . uh . . . I-I'm sorry," he said, stammering.

"Please answer the question."

"*Ah mur ch'churr jelusiar sha*," John gasped out, with a lump in his throat.

The rest of the examination was a blur to John. Somehow, he managed to answer every question, but as the cube clicked open after an hour, he had no idea whether his answers had been correct. It hardly seemed important now.

Emmie was waiting for him just outside the entrance to the examination hall, her face etched with worry. As soon as the Examiner had restored John's belongings, Emmie grabbed his arm and pulled him toward the TravelTube without saying a word.

A few minutes later they were sitting at a table on the grass in the Center, an enormous space that served the students as a huge park and a common room. Tall trees with leaves of green, gold, and yellow stretched toward the huge, transparent dome above. Several feet away, a small group of students splashed in the shallows of the lake. Most, however, walked past looking serious, their faces covered with white medical masks. News of the Zhaldarian Flu outbreak was all over the ship and, for once, the Center was practically empty. John stared up at the rings of balconies circling the vast space. Few of the stores and cafés had any customers.

John dropped his gaze, looking into Emmie's troubled eyes, unable to think of anything to say. They were both wrapped up in their own thoughts. John picked up the ham sandwich he had ordered from the food dispenser hut and nibbled a corner. With a sigh, he put it down again.

"He'll be okay, Emmie," he said, knowing it was a lie. "Kaal's going to be okay. Really. Dr. Kasaria —"

Emmie's head jerked up suddenly. "Oh no," she said, groaning. "Not him. Not now."

John turned around. Mordant Talliver was approaching their table across the grass, a smirk on his face. "Rats," he mumbled. "Keep cool, Emmie. You know he's going to try and get on our nerves."

Mordant stopped next to their table, G-Vez floating around his shoulders. "I heard your friend is feeling poorly, Riley," he said slyly. "How unfortunate that he has to miss exams. Maybe you two should try the same thing."

John's hands curled into fists beneath the table. Across from him, Emmie hissed sharply.

"Just say what you came to say and then get lost," John said between clenched teeth.

"What young Master Talliver is trying to tell you, is that —"

"Be quiet, G-Vez, I can speak for myself," snapped the half-Gargon boy.

"I am so terribly sorry, young sir. Please do carry on."

"I said shut up, stupid droid." Mordant batted the flashing metal ball away and turned back to John and Emmie. "As I was saying," he said with a sneer, "Maybe you'd both be better off if you followed your friend's example and spent the next few days in the medical wing instead of taking the rest of the exams."

"Are you saying Kaal's faking?" growled John, rising.

"John, keep cool. Remember what you just said," Emmie said.

Ignoring her, Mordant shrugged. "Whether he's faking or not, it's win-win, really," he said, gloating. "If your friend isn't faking, you've shared a room with him, so it's pretty much certain that you'll get Zhaldarian Flu, too. If he *is* faking, you still have to take the exams. You're bound to fail and get kicked out. Either way, I guess we won't be seeing you around here much longer."

"John, stop!" shouted Emmie.

Too late. John hurled himself across the table, fists swinging. The two boys went down in a tangle of arms, legs, and tentacles.

"Get off me!" Mordant shouted. "You'll give me your gross disease."

"You're a scumbag!" John choked as a thick, black tentacle curled around his neck. Another held him back. With sudden force, they were jerked apart.

"How very disappointing," said Doctor Graal.

Mordant unwound his tentacle from John's neck. Gasping, John stepped back from the glowering teacher as Mordant staggered to his feet.

"He started it!" yelped Mordant. "Tell her, G-Vez. John threw the first punch."

Doctor Graal interrupted before the small droid could speak. "I know what happened," she said. "I saw it all. You are very lucky I haven't called the Examiners." Turning from John to Mordant, her red eyes fiery, she went on, "Your Galactic Geography exam is tomorrow, and yet you are wasting your time fighting instead of studying. This is the sort of behavior we expect from primitive species, not Hyperspace High students."

"But Mordant said —" John began.

The Gargon teacher cut him off with a wave of her tentacle. "I am not interested in your arguments," she said in a haughty voice. "Go and study immediately, John Riley. There will be no special allowances just because your friend is ill."

CHAPTER 5

"Each of you will enter a simulation module and pilot a Class-II Training Dart through twelve solar systems, following the route laid in to your astrometric charts," barked Sergeant Jegger, strutting on three legs along the line of waiting students. Behind him were rows of t-dart simulation cockpits, which looked to John like large photo booths. Stopping at the center of the line, Jegger turned to face the class, his iron-gray mustache bristling. "Marks will be awarded for skillful avoidance of obstacles. The computer will also instruct you to land on a planet and take off again. Crashing your simulated ship means an immediate fail."

He paused for a second, peering at John through his two good eyes, the third hidden behind an eye patch. "Are you listening to me, Cadet Riley?"

"Sir, yes, sir," John replied briskly, groaning inwardly.

Since arriving on Hyperspace High, he had crashed twice. Nevertheless, Space Flight was one of the few exams that he felt confident he would pass.

The first crash had only happened because he had never before piloted a spaceship; the second because Mordant Talliver had made him lose control of a Xi-Class Privateer by playing chicken with John's craft. In spite of the two accidents, John had become an accomplished space pilot this term. Sergeant Jegger never let him forget the crashes but had told him, in his gruff manner, that he was "satisfied" with John's progress. In the entire class, John was now second only to Emmie in the cockpit of a spaceship.

"You will have two hours to complete your sweep," snapped Jegger, interrupting John's thoughts. "Points will be given for speed but deducted for reckless flying," he said, flashing a glance at Mordant.

"Sir," snapped Mordant.

The sergeant checked the time. "Enter your modules now. The simulation will commence in three point zero six minutes."

John climbed into one of the black cubes, looking around in surprise as the door shut behind him. Hyperspace High's level of technology was far beyond anything on Earth. If he hadn't known he was in a simulator, he would've thought it was a real ship. In front of him, the control panel adjusted to his height and reach. Outside of the cockpit was a perfect computer-generated view of Hyperspace High's main hangar deck. Before him were the bay doors that opened onto the vastness of space.

"Thirty seconds," Jegger said in his ear, as John pulled on his flying helmet. "It's only a simulation, cadets, but bring it back in one piece."

After the safety harness strapped him into his seat, John gripped the control stick.

"In three . . . two . . . one."

"Simulation begins," said the voice of the t-dart's computer. Ahead of John, the bay doors slid open.

"Preflight checks," John announced automatically.

"All systems verify ready."

"Astrometrics."

A 3-D chart of the galaxy appeared on an electronic display in the center of the control panel. Beside it, instructions scrolled past. John studied it for a moment. "Plot course for Tantarus Prime," he said, instructing the computer. "Take off on my mark."

Reaching out, John punched the power screen up to 500. The simulator module began to vibrate. Gripping the control stick, he pulled the stick backward gently. The t-dart's nose lifted off the deck.

"Mark," John said, flicking the flight button on top of the stick at the same moment.

In a roar of power, the training ship slammed through the open doors and into space.

"Takeoff executed. Course laid in," said the computer, as the little ship swept past the great bulk of Hyperspace High and out toward the stars.

Checking the astrometric screen, John adjusted his course, bringing the spaceship around until it was on a heading toward the first system on its tour. Satisfied, he tapped another screen. "Jump to hyperspace factor ten in three, two, one . . ." He hit another button. "Jump."

On the astrometric screen, John could see that he was already closing in on Tantarus Prime. He looked around himself, the thrill of space flight turning his skin to goose bumps. Although he was just flying a simulation, it felt exactly like he was speeding through space at a speed ten times faster than light. It was a sensation that was impossible to beat. *Better than any video game on Earth*, he thought. For a few moments, he even forgot about Kaal. Stars rushed past the cockpit as John said very quietly to himself: "Whoa."

The computer interrupted his thoughts. "Approaching Tantarus Prime."

John glanced at the screen. "Plot course for the Secundia Nebula," he instructed. Bringing the ship around gently, he commanded, "And increase speed to hyperspace factor two hundred."

A sudden grin appeared on his face. If points were being awarded for speed, he was going to try for every extra point he could get. Clutching the control stick tightly, John forgot about everything else, focusing on getting his ship around the course as quickly as possible.

"Asteroid field ahead," the computer told him twenty minutes later.

"At one thousand miles, drop out of

hyperspace," John replied. This, he knew, would be the first of many obstacles Jegger had plotted around the course.

The ship slowed. Smoothly, John moved the control stick, sending the tiny ship dodging past massive, spinning mountains of ice and rock like a robin diving for insects. A boulder filled his screen, hurtling toward him. Tensing, John jerked the stick, watching as the small asteroid sailed past, just a few feet away. A breath of relief escaped between his teeth in a slow hiss.

Jegger would've killed me if I crashed.

"Asteroid field cleared."

"Plot course for the L'Quara System and jump to hyperspace factor three hundred in three, two, one . . . jump."

Sergeant Jegger had plotted the course so that the students had to navigate through gigantic nebulae and clouds of gas, past black holes, and between blooming supernovas. Dropping out of hyperspace only when necessary and pushing the t-dart to higher and higher speeds whenever he had a clear run through space, John raced through the simulated galaxy.

"Make landing on planet Altore Three, then return to Hyperspace High," the computer told him eventually.

John tensed again. Landings were always nerve-racking. *Stay cool, John. You can do this in your sleep*, he thought. *Steady, steady . . .*

The t-dart hit the planet's atmosphere with a jolt. Decreasing speed, John checked his sensor displays. "Coming in too steep," he muttered, pulling the stick back slightly. The ship stabilized. Clouds whipped past the cockpit. As the t-dart drove through them into clear air, John scanned the planet's surface for a suitable landing space. He was descending over a vast, swirling ocean, but there was a dark mass of land off to his right. Vapor billowed from the ship's stubby wings. John turned, fingers jabbing at the screens once more.

"Prime jets, activate landing gear," he told the computer, as the craft roared over the coast. "Aaaaand, down."

Jets whining, the t-dart settled onto a featureless plain of grass.

"Landing executed."

John's fingers were already flickering over the screens ahead of him. A few seconds later, the t-dart burst through the Altore Three's atmosphere. "Lay in a course for Hyperspace High," John said quickly, "and jump to hyperspace on my command, maximum speed."

"Not bad, cadet. Not bad at all," said Sergeant Jegger, nodding approvingly as the door of John's simulator module opened a few minutes later. "One hour and thirty-four minutes."

"Am I the first back, sir?" John asked quickly, as he pulled off his helmet.

"That'll be the day," Emmie said snarkily, stepping out from behind Jegger and pushing her silver hair out of her eyes.

CHAPTER 6

The corner of Jegger's mouth twitched. "Tarz managed one hour thirty-three. Hardly anything in it," he said, almost smiling.

Even though Emmie looked pleased with her flight time, John could tell she was tired.

She's as worried about Kaal as I am, he thought sadly.

A few modules away, another door opened. Mordant stepped out, his face falling when he saw that Emmie and John had beaten him back. "Did you crash?" he asked, scowling.

"No," John snapped quickly. Desperate to get away from Mordant as quickly as possible, he turned back to Sergeant Jegger. "Do we need to stay here, sir?" he asked. "This is my last exam for the day, and I'd like to get up to the medical wing to see how Kaal's doing."

"And Professor Dibali has asked me to go to his study for some last-minute math tutoring," Emmie said.

Jegger nodded. "Dismissed," he said gruffly.

"I'm pretty sure I aced that," John whispered to Emmie as they hurried away. "Almost had a run-in with an asteroid, but that was the only problem."

"I did okay, too," Emmie replied, adding glumly, "the only exam I'm going to get a decent grade on."

The TravelTube door slid open. "You take this one," said Emmie. "Professor Dibali's office is at the other end of the ship from the medical wing, so I'll just slow you down. I'll see you in the library later. Give Kaal my love."

"Will do," said John, forcing a smile. *Even tired, Emmie looks pretty,* he thought. Her golden skin always looked radiant, but now it seemed to have an extra glow. A sheen of sweat glistened on her forehead. *Nerves,* John thought. "Kaal's going to be all right, Emmie," he said gently.

The Sillaran girl shook her head. "I wish I could believe that," she replied.

* * *

Dr. Kasaria spotted John as soon as he entered the medical wing. "John Riley," she said, rising from her desk. "I'm glad you're here.

I was going to ask you to return later. I received some interesting results from the tests I ran on you this morning."

John glanced through the clear screen into the quarantine room where Kaal lay motionless, hooked up to scary-looking machines and monitors. "I just came to visit Kaal," he said. "Would it be all right if I sat with him for a while?"

"I'm afraid not. As I said this morning, Zhaldarian Flu is extremely contagious. We cannot risk the infection spreading."

"But *you've* been in there," John blurted out. "Please, Dr. Kasaria. Please. Just for a little while?"

"It's for your own safety," the doctor said quietly. "Kaal's symptoms have grown worse. He has lost control of his limbs and parts of his brain. Zhaldarian Flu affects its victim's behavior. During this stage of the disease, Kaal is prone to violence."

"He'll be fine with me," John protested. "I'm his friend. He'd never hurt me."

Dr. Kasaria tilted her head on one side, regarding him with enormous black eyes. "For a few moments, then," she said eventually. "But you'll have to wear a protective suit and be accompanied by an Examiner. Afterward I want to run a few more tests on you."

Wearing white coveralls that shielded him from head to foot and a thicker face mask than the Examiners had handed out that morning, John followed an Examiner through the disinfectant field.

"Kaal," he said softly, moving toward the bed. "It's me, John. I just came to see how you're doing."

The Derrilian laid still. The only movement

was the rising and falling of his chest. John leaned over him. "Kaal. Can you hear me?"

Kaal's eyes blinked open.

"Hey, you're awake. How are you feeling?" John asked.

His friend's head turned. Eyes like red fire glared at John. "It was you. You did it," Kaal said, his voice hissing angrily.

"What? What are you talking about?" John asked.

"YOU PUT THE BRAINWEEVILS IN MY HEAD!" Kaal shouted, leaping from the bed. Tubes and wires snapped away from his arms. "THEY MAKE ME THINK OF . . . GAAH! THEY'RE HERE AGAIN."

John stepped back, shocked, as Kaal clawed at his own head. Out of the corner of his eye, he saw Dr. Kasaria rushing toward the disinfectant field.

"Kaal, you should get back into bed," John said.

"I'LL KILL YOU!" Kaal screamed, leaping toward John, his hands grabbing at the air.

"Easy, Kaal!" John shouted, leaping backward. But he was too slow. One of Kaal's hands gripped his throat. The other tore the mask from his face.

"YES, I CAN SEE YOU NOW, EMPEROR TAVARR —"

A green force field flung Kaal backward onto the bed. "Violence is prohibited," the Examiner droned in its electronic voice.

Dr. Kasaria caught John's arm as he staggered back. "Are you all right?" she asked quickly.

"I'm fine," John said, gasping. "What about Kaal?"

On the bed, Kaal thrashed and buckled,

screaming what John knew must be Derrilian swear words at the Examiner, since those were the only words the ship's computer did not translate.

"There is nothing I can do for the poor boy until he calms down," the doctor replied, pulling John back. "The Examiner will stop him from hurting himself until then. Now, John, come with me."

Looking over his shoulder at his tortured friend, John allowed Dr. Kasaria to guide him out of the quarantine room. Outside, Kaal's shouts and groans were muffled, but John could still hear him.

"You need to walk through the disinfectant portal," said the doctor. "You've been exposed again, and right now we need to take every precaution."

John removed his protective suit and did as

he was told. Once again, pink light wrapped around him as the machine puffed mist across his clothes and skin.

When he had finished, Kaal was still twisting and roaring on his bed. Dr. Kasaria watched him intently, her forehead creased in concern. She turned to John.

"Once I am able to get close enough, I'll give him some medicine to will make him sleep," she said. "I'll make him as comfortable as I possibly can, believe me."

John knew that beneath the doctor's brisk exterior, she cared deeply for Hyperspace High's students.

"I know," he replied simply.

"For you, there is good news," the doctor continued, her efficient manner returning. She pointed at the ThinScreen on her desk. What looked like a spiraling ladder was spinning in

3-D. "It seems that human DNA has some peculiarities."

"What sort of peculiarities?" John asked nervously.

"Well, for one, you appear to be completely immune to Zhaldarian Flu."

CHAPTER 7

John slouched away from the medical wing toward the TravelTube at the end of the corridor, hands in his pockets and a puzzled frown etched into his face. Even though Dr. Kasaria's news should have made him feel relieved, it just confused him.

Why were humans immune? He couldn't stop thinking about Kaal and what this sickness had done to him. He knew he should be hurrying to study, but after everything he had seen in the quarantine room he knew there was no way that he would be able to concentrate on Galactic Geography or Hyperspace History.

Pressing a panel to call the TravelTube, John sighed and ran his fingers through his hair.

A ball of light flashed through the wall at the end of the passage. It streamed toward him, trailing colored ribbons of light.

Stopping at his side, it morphed into the form of Lorem, the headmaster of Hyperspace High. Robed in white, he was an alien of medium height whose age John had never been able to guess.

Bald, and with the lined face of an old sage, Lorem's skin glimmered softly and his purple eyes twinkled with youth.

"Good evening, sir," John said politely.

"And to you, John Riley," the headmaster replied. "You've been to see Kaal?"

"Yes." John paused for a moment, feeling sadness well up. "He's . . . he's not doing so well."

"Zhaldarian Flu is a terrible disease, John," the headmaster replied softly.

John glanced up sharply as a thought occurred to him. Lorem had the ability to sense events that had yet to happen.

Quickly, John asked, "Have you looked into the future, sir? Do you know if . . . will Kaal get better?"

The headmaster looked back at him calmly. Crossing his arms, he replied. "As I have told you before, John, the shape of the future is not easy to see. There are many possible futures, each of which may or may not come to be, depending on the choices we all make. If different choices are made . . ." The headmaster shrugged. "Then the shape can change at any moment."

John's face fell. "So you can't tell?" he asked flatly.

Uncrossing his arms, Lorem said enigmatically, "Choices, John. Choices."

John shook his head, even more confused than before.

Lorem patted him on the shoulder and said, "Nothing is ever certain, but a certain train of events is possible. A train of events that gives me hope." Lorem smiled at John, and continued briskly, "But for now, I suggest you eat and rest. Flu or no flu, you have a Hyperspace History exam tomorrow. Now, if you will excuse me, I am on my way to visit Kaal."

In front of John the TravelTube door slid open. "Yes, sir," he said. "And if there's anything I can do . . ."

"I know, John," said Lorem, disappearing in a flash of light.

A few minutes later, John took his usual seat in the Center. Kaal's place next to him was empty and so, too, was Emmie's. *Probably still with Professor Dibali,* he told himself, deciding not to wait for her.

"I could use some comfort food today, Zepp," he said into empty air. "Chicken pot pie and mashed potatoes with gravy would be great, please."

Lishtig plunked himself down in the seat across the table. "Hi, John. Jegger said you'd gone to visit Kaal. How is he?"

The hulking Gobi-san-Art settled his huge, rocky frame in the seat next to Lishtig. "Can he talk? Did he say anything?" he asked in his deep voice.

Next to John, the thin, gray Bareon sat down. Fixing John with eyes almost as big as Dr. Kasaria's, he asked softly, "What are his symptoms?"

"Kaal's not so great," John said quickly. He didn't want to dwell on just how sick his friend was; he knew that wouldn't help. At that moment four steaming bowls slid out of the food dispenser.

"What's this?" he said, looking into a bowl of pink mush with green blobs floating in it.

"Ew," said Lishtig, sniffing his bowl. "Smells like something the Sklart dragged in."

Gobi dipped a spoon into his bowl, letting the mush drop back in with a wet squelch. "I've had exams all day and I'm exhausted — don't you have anything better than this to eat, Zepp?" he complained.

"Tonight's meal is an automatic selection," the ship's computer replied. "It is Vita-Soup. Please finish the bowl."

"Vita-Soup," said John, wrinkling his nose. "It looks more like Vita-Goop."

Bareon, whose father was a medic with the Galactic Fleet, did his best to explain. "Vita-Soup is a specially engineered foodstuff that can be eaten by all known life forms in the universe," he said. "It contains all the vitamins and minerals necessary to build up the immune system." He paused for a moment before slurping a spoonful. "And it tastes absolutely disgusting," he finished glumly.

John almost choked on his first mouthful. "I'd rather eat my own toenails," he said, letting his spoon fall into his bowl. "Chicken pot pie's got lots of vitamins and minerals, too, you know, Zepp," he added hopefully.

"I'm sorry, John. Headmaster's orders," Zepp replied.

An Examiner floated to the table, lights blinking across its smooth, white head. "All students must finish the Vita-Soup," it droned. "Failure to comply will result in detention and double Vita-Soup rations tomorrow."

"I thought the infection had been contained," said Gobi, groaning. He picked up his spoon again. "Why are we being forced to eat this mush if there's no chance we could get the flu anyway?"

Bareon forced down another mouthful, his face twisting in disgust. "Yuck . . . Zhaldarian Flu is extremely contagious," he replied. "And very serious. I had a great-great-great-great-great uncle who died from it." Hearing John gasp, he turned around. "Sorry, John . . . I didn't mean to worry you . . . that was hundreds of years ago. Treatments have improved since then. I'm sure Kaal will be —"

"It's okay," said John, raising a hand to stop Bareon's apology.

Lishtig and Gobi changed the subject, asking John about the Space Flight exam. John answered politely, but finished the soup as quickly as he could. "Got to meet Emmie in the library for studying," he said, as he gulped down the last spoonful. "I'll see you guys in the morning."

John rushed to the library, but there was no sign of Emmie. *Dibali must be working her hard,* he thought, as he sat at an empty desk. For half an hour, he tried to concentrate on Hyperspace History, but his mind kept wandering back to Kaal. As the minutes ticked by and Emmie still hadn't arrived, he began to worry a little. "It's nothing. She's always late," he said to himself.

As half an hour turned into an hour, his worry grew. Unable to put his finger on why he was anxious, John sat back in his MorphSeat and cast his mind back to the last time he had seen her. She was fine, wasn't she? Emmie had looked tired, but she had been perfectly healthy. Her skin even had a glow to it.

Just like Kaal's.

CHAPTER 8

"Emmie left here over an hour ago," said a confused Professor Dibali a few minutes later.

John looked up into the math teacher's eyes, which weaved about at the end of long stalks. "Did she happen to mention where she was going, sir?"

"I'm sorry, no. But she looked a little tense. Perhaps she went to one of the gyms to do some exercise."

Anxiety mounting, John sprinted down the corridor toward the TravelTube. He checked every gym on the ship, which took another twenty-five minutes. Still there was no sign of Emmie.

It's okay. Emmie's okay. Her golden skin always looks like it's glowing.

John ran around the balconies of the Center, asking every student he passed if they had seen her.

"Sillaran girl? Silver hair?" said a third year with patched, harlequin skin and a flickering forked tongue.

"That's her," John said, panting from his frantic search.

"Not sure," said the third year, "but I may have passed her a while ago on the way to the chemistry labs."

"Thanks!" John called over his shoulder,

racing away again. They had a chemistry exam after the Hyperspace History test the next day, and it was possible Emmie had gone to check an experiment or to get some extra help.

"Chemistry laboratories," said the TravelTube. John was out of the door before it had finished opening.

Before him was one of the strangest corridors on the ship. Every wall, along with the ceiling, was made from long glass tubes, each filled with a different-colored, bubbling liquid.

As Professor Shard, the chemistry teacher, liked to often remind the class, in her science laboratories, even the walls were part of the experiments.

Taking no time to marvel over the strange sights, John peered into rooms filled with enormous crystal structures and laboratories where tiny suns burned in protective jars. A few students looked up from their work as he entered the labs, but there was no sign of Emmie anywhere.

In the last room almost all the space was taken up by a fantastically complex arrangement of force fields, holding a single drop of antimatter securely in place.

As John poked his head around the door, his heart leaped. Standing at a ThinScreen was a girl with silver hair.

But when she turned around, his heart sank. This girl had turquoise skin, as well as an extra pair of eyes.

"Where is she?" he muttered to himself, as he raced back to the TravelTube.

One after another, he checked Emmie's favorite places. The movie theater complex was closed until the flu scare had passed. The music rooms were empty, apart from Mistress Soo-See, who was playing a sad melody on an Operian harp on the floating stage of the concert hall. The ornately carved instrument stretched one hundred feet above her head.

Everywhere he went John was met with blank looks. Finally, breathing heavily, he leaned against the wall. He mentally retraced his steps, wondering if there was anywhere he could have missed.

To the astonishment of two passing students, he suddenly slapped his own forehead. "I'm such an idiot," he told them, running off again as they stared.

Diving into a TravelTube, he cried, "Dormitory level sixteen."

He made it to Emmie's floor and ran to her room.

"Emmie!" John shouted, pressing the

doorbell and banging on the door of her room. "Open up! It's me, John."

There was no answer. John pressed his ear to the door.

There was silence within.

"EMMIE!" he bellowed at the top of his lungs. Around the lobby, students turned to see what the commotion was about.

Still no answer.

"This is no time to worry about privacy," he muttered to himself. Raising his voice again, he shouted, "Emmie, I'm coming in!" He put his hand to a panel.

The door slid open.

And John dropped to his knees, a sob in his throat.

Emmie had collapsed on the floor, her skin glowing with golden light. As John watched in dismay, she suddenly shifted position. Pulling her knees up to her chest, she wrapped her arms around them and groaned.

CHAPTER 9

"Zepp!" John yelled. "Meteor Medics to Emmie's room, NOW. She has the flu."

It took a second for the computer to reply. "No Meteor Medics are available at this moment," it said.

"None? What about Examiners?" John asked frantically.

"All Examiners are currently occupied," the computer said.

"All of them?" John said, shocked. "What on Earth is going on?"

"Zhaldarian Flu has spread. Hyperspace High's emergency systems are at full capacity."

John cursed under his breath. He had to get Emmie to Dr. Kasaria, and there was no time to waste.

That left only one option. Slipping his arms beneath Emmie, he cradled her to his chest and lifted her. She was hot, her skin slippery with sweat, but she was easy to carry.

For a moment John wondered how his friend, who was always so full of energy and surprisingly strong, could weigh so little. Holding her tenderly, he quickly raced out of her dorm room. "Stay away. Get back to your rooms!" he shouted at the students who were still chatting in the lobby. "Get out of my way. Move! She's contagious."

The hall cleared in seconds. Clasping Emmie tightly, John carried her to the TravelTube. "Medical wing," he said. "Fast."

The elevator shot sideways. John lurched on his feet, half-turning to protect his friend from slamming into the wall.

"Emmie," he said, his voice cracking. "Can you hear me? You're going to be all right. I'm taking you to Dr. Kasaria. She'll make you feel better."

Emmie's eyelids flickered. For a split second, her navy blue eyes, full of pain, looked up at him. "John," she whispered. "I'm not feeling so . . ." Her voice trailed off, and her eyes closed again.

John was already calling for Dr. Kasaria as the TravelTube door opened. Bellowing for help, he raced through the doors to the medical wing and skidded to a halt.

Hover stretchers were floating everywhere, each one occupied by an unconscious student. Through the clear screen, John could see the quarantine ward had been enlarged massively. Now, Kaal lay in the first of a long line of beds. Meteor Medics rushed from one patient to the next, their thin metal fingers glinting under the lights as they took samples and scanned every new arrival.

Dr. Kasaria stalked through the chaos, stopping every so often to comfort the patients that were still conscious. Her hands touched complicated medical computers while she gave instructions to the Meteor Medics in her efficient tone. "Make sure all patients are securely strapped down," she told them. "We cannot risk them attacking each other."

As quickly as new patients were moved into beds, even more patients arrived. Behind John, a line of hover stretchers was forming, each carrying another Zhaldarian Flu victim.

"Dr. Kasaria!" John called. "Come here, please! I need help."

The doctor glanced at him and then down at Emmie in his arms. "The poor girl," she murmured. Then she was all efficiency again. "Carry her to an empty bed, John," she said. "We will see to her soon."

"Can't I stay? There's got to be something I can do."

"No, you'll get in the way." The doctor turned away, already issuing new instructions as she took the pulse of a red-skinned boy whose chin reached to his waist. "We need more beds," she said briskly. "Zepp, can you help?"

"There are some in storage, Dr. Kasaria," the computer answered immediately. "I will have the droids bring them up."

"Carry her to an empty bed and then get back to your dormitory, John," Dr. Kasaria repeated over her shoulder.

John laid Emmie on one of the few empty beds. Gently wiping her face with a cool cloth, he whispered, "You're the strongest person I know, Emmie. Don't let this sickness beat you."

* * *

There was no music when Zepp woke John up the next morning. In a grave voice, the computer told him that more than one hundred cases of Zhaldarian Flu had been reported. "Examiners have left quarantine suits outside every dormitory. You are to wear yours at all times."

"But Dr. Kasaria said I'm immune," John said, protesting.

"You may be carrying Zhaldarian Flu germs," Zepp replied. "The suit will stop you from spreading them."

In silence, John washed his face. Without Kaal, the dormitory seemed big and lifeless. In an attempt to fill the emptiness, he flicked on the entertainment ThinScreen.

". . . reports are reaching us describing an outbreak of Zhaldarian Flu on Hyperspace High," said a two-headed news reporter. "The first outbreak of the killer disease for more than two hundred years. Lorem, the school's headmaster, has confirmed that more than a hundred students have been diagnosed with the disease. The Galactic Council has sent an emergency team of Meteor Medics to the school and placed it under strict quarantine. A fleet has surrounded the famous school under the command of Councillor Tarz, whose own daughter is among the flu victims. Any unauthorized ship approaching or leaving Hyperspace High will be destroyed . . ."

Clicking the screen off, John opened the door. Outside was a neat package with the words "QUARANTINE SUIT" printed on the wrapping.

As the door slid closed, he pulled off the cover, revealing a large lump of what looked like clear jelly.

"What's this, Zepp?" he asked, confused. He had been expecting some sort of surgical suit, not a jellylike blob.

"Put your hand inside to activate the suit," the computer instructed him.

John wriggled his fingers into the rubbery lump. At his touch, it seemed to come alive. Wide-eyed, he watched as the clear rubber crawled up his arm, quickly spreading across his chest and down his legs, leaving them covered in a thin gel.

When it reached his face, he almost panicked, raising his hands to pull the creeping material away.

"Stay still," Zepp told him as the rubbery stuff covered his mouth. "It will allow you to breathe, but filter the air so that no infections can get in or out. In a few moments you won't even know you're wearing it."

"I'm not so sure about that," said John, blinking as the quarantine suit formed bubbles like swimming goggles over his eyes.

But Zepp was right. The suit was clear and weightless. John could breathe normally and see perfectly. He looked in the mirror. His usually tousled hair was pressed down flat against his head, but besides that it was pretty hard to tell that he was even wearing the quarantine suit.

"What about eating?" he asked, pulling his school uniform on over the top of the quarantine suit. The elastic gel stretched over his mouth as he spoke.

"The suit is semi-intelligent," Zepp replied. "Nano-sensors detect when you wish to eat, and the suit will create an opening around your mouth. But now, John, on the subject of food, I do suggest you go to the Center. Your Hyperspace History exam begins in less than half an hour."

"No way!" gasped John. "There's a flu epidemic. You said yourself that people are dropping in the halls."

"The headmaster has said that the school routine will continue as normal for those not affected by the flu."

A strange stillness had settled over

Hyperspace High. As John walked from the dormitory level to the Center, he met a few quarantine-suited students talking in whispers in the corridors, but there was none of the usual lively chatter.

Twice, he saw students collapse. Their friends sobbed quietly, as Meteor Medics came and quickly carried the new victims off on hover stretchers.

Approaching the Center, John caught a glimpse through the viewing window of the emergency medical ship the Galactic Council had sent.

The bulky gray craft, piloted by and only carrying robots, had docked against one of Hyperspace High's wings.

At least there are plenty of Meteor Medics on board now, he told himself, remembering what he'd seen in the understaffed medical wing the night before.

After eating his bowl of Vita-Soup, John followed Lishtig, Bareon, and Gobi-san-Art to the examination hall, feeling oddly calm. This time he had no butterflies in his stomach. With Emmie and Kaal both sick and staff and students collapsing around him, the exams seemed irrelevant.

Many of the examination cubes were empty. John noticed with a sinking heart that another of his classmates — Raytanna — was missing. John knew it had to be the flu — only serious illness would stop studious Raytanna from taking an exam. He took his seat quietly. In the next cube, Bareon looked thoughtful. Next to him, Lishtig had lost his usual good-natured grin.

"Examination commences," the computer suddenly announced. John's attention snapped to the ThinScreen on the small desk ahead of him. "You have one hour. Identify the following historical events and place them in chronological order."

An image flashed onto the screen: a desert battle between orange-skinned lizard creatures and what looked like flying jellyfish. "The Arvuna War; six point seven six two Galactic Era," said John automatically. Reaching out, he touched the screen, making the image smaller and dragging it into a slot on a grid.

As image followed after image, John's concentration increased. The test was a welcome escape from thinking about Zhaldarian Flu and his friends in the medical wing. "The Palace of Galactic Unity is completed . . ." He paused, unable to remember exactly when the vast building with its elegant silver spires had been built.

He dragged it to a space in the grid. As he did so, he glanced at the clock in the corner of the screen, realizing with a jolt that there were only twenty minutes left until the exam finished. More than half the grid still remained to be filled.

"Come on, John," he muttered to himself. "If you get thrown out of here, you'll never see Kaal and Emmie again."

As quickly as he could, John placed more images. Beads of sweat broke out on his forehead when he realized he had put the Arvuna War after the coronation of Shim Emperor R'eshed the Unholy. His fingers flickered across the screen as he rearranged the order.

Five minutes left, he reminded himself, looking in horror at the many blank spaces. John heard a thump on the clear wall next to him. He spun around. Bareon was standing, clutching his triangular head in his long, gray fingers, and was staggering around inside his cube.

In an instant, John had kicked open the door to his own cube. "Ms. Vartexia," he yelled at the Elvian teacher supervising the exam. "Call the Meteor Medics. It's Bareon —"

"Stay calm, I will deal with the emergency," the tall, blue-skinned teacher replied. Louder, she called out, "Meteor Medics to examination hall eight immediately."

By now, other students were standing outside their cubes. More doors opened.

"All of you, finish your exam," Ms. Vartexia ordered. "Help is on its way."

But John didn't take any notice. He tore open the door to Bareon's cube. Staggering out, the triangular-headed boy collapsed into his arms.

Meteor Medics rushed into the room.

John gazed down at the flickering eyelids of the boy in his arms.

Who cares about that stupid test anymore? he thought.

Bareon groaned.

"Don't worry," said John.

A bell sounded. Holding up Bareon, John glanced over his shoulder. On the ThinScreen in his cubicle, the grid — with all its blank spaces — disappeared.

The test was over.

John knew that he had probably flunked his history exam. But the lives of his friends were at stake.

It wasn't just his time at Hyperspace High

that could be coming to an end — the Zhaldarian

Flu might signal the end of the school forever.

CHAPTER 10

Certain that his stay at Hyperspace High would soon be over, John was determined to spend as much time as he could with his best friends. He pushed through the crowd of students and followed the hover stretcher that was rushing Bareon to the medical wing.

There, John found that the situation had grown worse since the night before. In the corridor, beings from all across the universe were curled up on hover stretchers, glowing gently.

After pausing to lay a hand on Bareon's shoulder, he made his way through the hover stretchers, recognizing several patients — Tarope, a frog-like being with orange skin who had been on John's Galactic Battle team a few weeks earlier, and Emmie's roommate, Queelin Temerate, the stubby feelers on her forehead drooping.

Inside the medical wing, the scene was even more chaotic. By the entrance, the black bulk of Doctor Graal lay on a stretcher, a dark red glow shimmering across her skin, her tentacles wrapped tightly around herself.

Dr. Kasaria was leaning over the Gargon teacher, her forehead lined with strain as she took a sample of black blood.

"Zepp!" she called out, passing a hand across her brow. "This is the last patient we can fit in here. Is there any room available on the ship where we can open an emergency ward? Anything at all?"

"Affirmative," Zepp's voice replied. "The headmaster asked for the 4-D movie theater to be prepared."

"Good," said the doctor quickly. "Is it ready?"

"Droids are setting up beds now. I have established a quarantine zone."

"Excellent," said the doctor, standing straight and waving over an Examiner. "Redirect new patients to the 4-D movie theater," she told the white robot. "I will follow soon." Spotting John by the door, she said briskly, "What are you doing here again? As you can see, we are very busy."

"Sorry to disturb you, Dr. Kasaria," John replied. "I was hoping to check in on Kaal and Emmie . . ."

His voice trailed off as he saw the glare that the doctor was giving him. A glare that told him that she didn't have time to look after visitors. He blushed and shuffled his feet.

Seeing the look of concern on his face, Dr. Kasaria's narrow shoulders slumped. "I'm sorry, John," she said, sounding weary. "Of course you are worried about your friends. Please just wait here. I will be back once I have Doctor Graal settled."

John found a small corner of the medical wing that wasn't crammed with hover stretchers and stood quietly while Meteor Medics began moving patients back through the doors, heading for the new emergency ward.

Through the clear screen, he watched Dr.

Kasaria push the Gargon teacher into the quarantine ward. The room was now packed with beds. Many of the patients were straining against the straps that held them down, screaming.

An Examiner used its force fields to move Graal into the last remaining bed, while the doctor reset monitors and began inserting tubes into the Gargon teacher's tentacles.

Soon, the medical wing's reception room had emptied. John looked around as the door hissed open again, expecting to see a Meteor Medic.

Instead, he found himself face-to-face with a grim-looking Mordant Talliver, G-Vez bobbing, as usual, around his shoulders.

John blinked in surprise. He didn't look sick, but it was difficult to imagine that Mordant

Talliver cared enough about anyone to visit the medical wing.

Maybe he's here to see Emmie. John scowled as the thought occurred to him. He had always suspected that Mordant had a crush on his beautiful friend.

The half-Gargon boy constantly picked on Emmie and tried to bully her. John had seen the same behavior at school on Earth and knew that bullies often had feelings for their targets that they were too ashamed to admit. *Although,* thought John, *that doesn't explain why Mordant is always so horrible to me.*

For a moment the two boys stared at each other. Mordant obviously hadn't expected to find John there either. He took a step backward.

"What are you doing here?" John asked in an icy voice.

Mordant simply stared back at him, his face blank.

"If you're trying see Emmie, you can get lost."

"What makes you think that young Master Talliver would wish to visit the Sillaran," G-Vez drawled in its electronic voice. "No. In fact, he has come to —"

"Shut up, G-Vez," snapped Mordant.

G-Vez said, "I wished only to correct the Earthling's idea that you, of all people, would want to see —"

"I said, shut up. Now."

"So, why are you here?" John repeated. "You don't look sick."

Mordant took a sharp breath. Turning on his heel, he walked back through the door.

John stared in surprise as Mordant strode

away. Normally, the black-haired boy would never have let a chance to insult John slip by, but today, he had walked away without saying a word.

For a moment, John felt a pang of guilt, wondering if he had misjudged Mordant. Then he remembered the boy's glee while taunting him and Emmie about Kaal's illness.

Nope. I didn't misjudge him. Same old jerk, same old Mordant. He probably just came up here to point and laugh at all the sick people, John thought. *Typical Mordant.*

"John?" Dr. Kasaria's voice startled him.

"What's going on?" he asked. "Is something wrong with Kaal and Emmie? I mean, are they worse . . . ?"

"Emmie is stable," Dr. Kasaria said softly, gazing at him gently with her large, black eyes.

"I have every hope that she will eventually recover."

A chill gripped John's heart. "And Kaal?" he whispered.

The doctor sighed. "The Zhaldarian Flu seems to have mutated. Kaal is displaying symptoms that I have never seen before. None of the normal treatments are working. His condition is critical. I have moved him to another room."

"What symptoms? How critical? He's going to get better, isn't he?" John blurted out.

The doctor rested a hand on his shoulder and squeezed. "Would you like to see him?" she asked.

John gulped and nodded.

"Since you are immune and wearing a full quarantine suit, it cannot do any harm," Dr.

Kasaria said. "The aggressive stage of the disease has passed. Kaal is in a coma, but it is possible that he can still hear what is going on around him. If so, I'm sure it would be a comfort for him to hear your voice. Follow me."

Shaking, John followed as the doctor led him along a hallway lined with doors that led onto smaller, private rooms. Each held a single patient with a Meteor Medic hovering by his or her bed.

Without being told, John knew that these were the most serious cases.

At the end of the corridor, the doctor paused. "Try and stay positive. Kaal cannot speak but if he can hear you, it is better if he doesn't know how worried we are."

John nodded again. Dr. Kasaria placed her hand on a wall panel. The door slid open.

John walked quickly past the Meteor Medic by the bed and looked down at his roommate.

More tubes had been inserted into Kaal's flesh. An oxygen mask covered his face. John had to force himself not to step back. Even from a few feet away, he could feel the heat rising from his friend's body. Kaal's normally bulging muscles looked as if they had deflated. His skin hung loose and, as John watched, it began to change color, turning from green to a violent shade of red. The only sounds in the room were the hissing of oxygen and hushed beeps from a bank of monitors.

John reached out and put a quarantine-suited hand on Kaal's arm, feeling burning skin through the gel. "All right, pal?" he said, trying to make his voice sound as cheerful as possible. "You missed a really tough exam today . . ."

Kaal remained completely still and silent

as John talked. The only signs of life were the constantly changing colors of his skin and the rising and falling of his chest as oxygen was pumped into his lungs. John forced himself to go on, keeping his voice cheerful — even as he realized that his best friend was dying.

CHAPTER 11

John talked and talked, hardly taking time to draw breath, his gaze fixed on Kaal's face. He talked about the fun they would have playing their virtual-reality games when Kaal recovered, about their adventures on Zirion Beta and Archivus Major, winning the Robot Warriors' competition, visiting the scholars of Kerallin, and the deadly battle they fought at the Space Spectacular.

"It's been a really intense couple of months," he told his friend. "Let's hope we can get through next semester without being in grave danger every five minutes."

He paused for a moment, and then continued quietly, "That's if I make it back next semester. I totally messed up the Hyperspace History exam."

For the first time, Kaal's eyelids flickered. John leaned forward. "Kaal?" he whispered. "Can you hear me?"

The Meteor Medic floated forward. "VISIT TERMINATED," it said.

"But he can hear me," said John. "His eyes moved. I'm getting through to him."

"LEAVE IMMEDIATELY," the droid

droned, "OR THE EXAMINERS WILL BE INFORMED."

There was no choice but to leave. Telling Kaal he would be back as soon as possible, John walked out of the isolation room and into the reception area.

It was empty now. He paused, guessing that the doctor had gone to the new emergency ward in the 4-D movie theater.

Turning, John looked through the screen to the quarantine ward. Emmie lay on a bed near the far end of the room, her fearful eyes staring up at the ceiling.

As he watched, a pale blue tear ran down her cheek.

John felt his heart lurch in his chest.

Dr. Kasaria never said I couldn't visit Emmie, too, he told himself, already moving toward the disinfectant field that led to the ward. *I won't disturb anyone; I'll just spend a few minutes with her.*

"STOP," droned an electronic voice behind him. "RULE NUMBER FIVE-ZERO-FOUR: NO STUDENT IS TO ENTER THE QUARANTINE WARD."

Unseen by John, an Examiner had floated through the medical wing's main doors.

But John didn't stop. "It's okay!" he called over his shoulder. "Dr. Kasaria knows I'm here and I'm immune, there's no dang—"

A haze of green appeared around John, holding him in place, one foot through the disinfectant field.

"RULE NUMBER ZERO-ZERO-EIGHT-THREE: EXAMINERS ARE TO BE OBEYED AT ALL TIMES. PUNISHMENT FOR NON-COMPLIANCE —"

A ball of light flashed through the wall and sparkled into the form of the headmaster. "I will deal with this," Lorem said sternly.

The force field flicked off. Able to move again, John turned to face Lorem. The headmaster looked grave.

Uh-oh, I'm in trouble now.

"Take a walk with me, John," Lorem said, striding toward the door.

The tone of his voice made John's feet start moving before Lorem had even finished his sentence.

"I just wanted to see Emmie, sir," he explained, as he followed the headmaster out into the corridor. "I wasn't going to stay very long . . ."

Lorem raised his hand, and John immediately stopped talking, walking in silence as the white-robed headmaster turned and strode along an empty corridor that ended at one of Hyperspace High's observation decks.

Ignoring the comfortable MorphSeats, Lorem crossed the floor, standing at the edge of the deck. John knew that a transparent dome surrounded them, but, even so, he had to stop himself from lunging forward to drag the headmaster out of danger.

It seemed as if he were standing on the very edge of space. Nervously, John joined him, standing by his side and looking out at the glittering clusters of stars.

For a few heartbeats, neither spoke. Eventually, John cleared his throat and said, "I'm sorry. I thought it might make Emmie feel better to see a friend."

Lorem looked down at him. "Don't worry

about that," he said kindly. "I would have done the same thing in your position. Still, it is never a good idea to disobey the Examiners. Next time wait for Dr. Kasaria to return and ask permission." The headmaster turned back to watching the stars.

"So, I'm . . . uhh . . . not going to be punished?"

"John, I sense how troubled you are by your friends' illness," the headmaster said. "You know, I understand exactly how you feel. You don't know this, but when I was a young boy, many centuries ago, my best friend contracted Zhaldarian Flu. I still remember how helpless I felt watching him suffer."

"What happened to your friend?" asked John. "He got better, right?"

Lorem shook his head, his purple eyes filled

with sorrow. "I'm sorry to say that he didn't make it."

"But you said that you'd seen the future. Isn't everything going to be okay?"

"I said that I hope one possible future will come to pass, but, as I told you, it depends on the choices that certain people will make." Lorem continued, "It was thought that Zhaldarian Flu had been wiped out over two hundred years ago after the entire universe had been vaccinated against it. There hasn't been a single case in all that time. However, it appears that Doctor Graal opened a box containing a rock sample from Zhaldaria in class a few days ago. The sample was infected."

John's eyes widened as he remembered Kaal reaching out to touch Doctor Graal's precious rock sample in their Galactic Geography class.

"All this suffering is Doctor Graal's fault, then?" he asked. He couldn't keep the anger from his voice.

"Do not be so quick to judge, John," the headmaster replied, holding up one finger. "I know you dislike Doctor Graal, but it was not her fault."

"If she had checked before she opened the box, Kaal wouldn't be fighting for his life . . . sir."

Lorem sighed, thinking it over. "No one has thought much about Zhaldarian Flu for two centuries. Most planets have stopped vaccinating their children against it. Everyone believed that it had been eradicated completely, and there was no way Doctor Graal could have known," he said. "Would you have thought to check a tiny rock sample for an ancient disease?"

John's shoulders slumped. "There's no cure, then?" he said eventually, shaking his head. "We just have to wait and see who survives and who dies?"

With a solemn nod, the headmaster said, "We know how to produce an effective vaccine, but once the disease has taken hold there is nothing anyone can do. We will keep the patients as comfortable as possible and treat their symptoms, but there is no known cure." He paused for a moment, then continued thoughtfully, "Though I have been doing some research. My friend Scholar Aristil, who you met on Kerallin, tells me that just before Zhaldarian Flu disappeared, a group of scientists on Gwaterra Four claimed that they had discovered certain microbes that could cure the disease."

John felt a surge of hope rising in his chest.

"Wait a second," he said. "There's a cure? Can we get some?"

For a moment, Lorem's eyes sparkled with their usual brilliance. But it faded so quickly John thought he might have imagined it.

Wearily, the headmaster replied, "Zhaldarian Flu vanished soon after they made their discovery. Other scientists challenged the Gwaterrans' findings and, with no patients to test their theory on, it remains uncertain whether the microbes are an effective cure."

"It must be worth a try, though," John said eagerly.

The headmaster nodded slowly. "Perhaps. But the microbes are very rare. They only exist in the core of the Zaleta Nebula. The Gwaterrans thought that when Zhaldaria's star exploded, destroying the planet, the radiation changed the structure of the flu virus, creating a new strain that adapted to live at the heart of a nebula. According to their theory, these new microbes would cure the disease they originally created. Microbes that can dwell in such a hostile environment are unheard of, but if they do exist it is likely that they would have highly unusual properties."

"If we know where they are, why hasn't anyone gone to find some?" John asked with a frown.

"Because it is an extremely dangerous task. The microbes are very delicate and would only be found in the hot gases at the very core of the nebula. No robot has ever successfully made the trip — their circuits have all been scrambled by radioactive interference. The only possible way would be if someone were brave enough to dive to the center of the nebula and collect the microbes by hand."

"But someone has to try," John replied bluntly. "People will die if they don't, headmaster. Don't you —"

"I have contacted the Galactic Council," Lorem declared. "No one is willing to take a chance on an unproven hypothesis."

"Then someone from Hyperspace High?"

The headmaster shook his head again. "During an emergency, the priority for staff is to look after sick students. There are few enough of us left as it is."

"A student, then. Why couldn't a student go?"

Seconds ticked by as the headmaster stood, looking at John in silence.

Finally, he spoke, his voice more serious than John had ever heard it before. "The Galactic

Council would never allow me to send a student

on such a dangerous mission."

"Then what can we do?"

"We can wait, John. Wait and hope."

CHAPTER 12

As the headmaster turned into a ball of light and zipped away, John remained where he was, staring out into space with his hands in his pockets.

Somewhere out there might be a cure for Emmie and Kaal.

A strand of blond hair fell into his eyes. He pushed it away and blinked. "Zepp?"

"Yes, John," replied the computer's calm voice.

"Would a human being be able to withstand . . . no, actually, never mind," John said. "It doesn't matter."

He sighed. Telling his thoughts to the ship's computer was a sure way of inviting failure before his plan was even fully formed. Zepp would be duty-bound to tell on him.

"Very well," Zepp replied. "If you need help, just let me know."

John pulled his ThinScreen from his bag. His fingers tapped across it, delving into the wafer-thin computer's almost limitless data banks until he found what he was looking for. His eyes fixed on the screen, he began walking toward the nearest TravelTube, fingers moving deftly as he searched for more information and boarded the elevator.

"Dormitory level sixteen."

John tucked the ThinScreen back into his bag as the door slid open onto the common room area outside the dormitories.

At this time of day, it was usually buzzing with conversation as students relaxed between classes. Now, it was virtually empty. Dol, Kritta, and Werril were sitting by the fountain in the middle of the room, talking in hushed voices. Several feet beyond them, Mordant Talliver was slumped in a MorphSeat, staring into space in stony silence, his Serve-U-Droid hovering silently beside him.

"Are you immune, too?" asked dolphin-like Dol as John approached.

John nodded. "So Dr. Kasaria says. And you?"

"Yes. There are a few of us and some, like

Kritta, who were vaccinated against Zhaldarian Flu. Some planets still do it."

"Thank goodness," Kritta said, clicking her insect-like mouthparts with feeling.

"Is anyone else left?" John asked, hoping there were other students unaffected. Although he liked the three of them, he needed help and none of them were well suited to the task he had in mind.

"We're the only first years," said Werril, nervously rubbing the horn that sprouted from the middle of his face. "There are a few older students scattered around, but another flu wave went through the ship like a hurricane about an hour ago. Lishtig's down with it now, Gobi . . . everyone."

John crossed his arms. "Okay, then I need one of you guys to help me."

Kritta turned her enormous compound eyes on him. "Help you do what?"

As quickly as possible, John repeated what the headmaster had said about the microbes at the center of the Zaleta Nebula. "I checked it out," he explained to them. "With the right protection, I should be able to withstand the environment in the middle of the nebula for about thirty minutes. There are nebula-diving pods in the main hangar. All I need is for someone to fly the ship while I go in and get what we need."

Three faces stared at him in confusion. John stared back at them.

"You want to steal a ship, fly to the Zaleta Nebula, and go looking for microbes that may or may not have any effect on the Zhaldarian Flu?" Kritta asked after a few moments.

"And probably kill yourself in the process," added Werril.

"If we don't try, our friends are going to die," John said, hoping one of them would rise to the challenge.

"They'll probably die anyway," Werril pointed out. "There's no proof these microbes will help."

"But they might work," John replied quickly. "It's got to be worth the risk."

"I don't think so," Werril said, taking a step backward. "You'd never manage to get off Hyperspace High. And even if you did, it's a completely crazy plan."

"Listen to Werril," Dol said. "It's madness. Besides, Lorem said himself that he could never allow you to risk your life."

"No," John replied quietly. "He said the

Galactic Council would never allow it. He also said that the choices we make could change the future."

"You're hearing what you want to hear, John," Kritta said gently. "The headmaster didn't mean that you should fly off and get yourself killed."

John looked from face to face to face. It was already obvious that none of his classmates were willing to risk their lives. Nevertheless, they were his only hope. He would never get to the Zaleta Nebula and back on his own.

"Think of Kaal," he pleaded with Kritta, who he knew had a soft spot for his friend. "We have to try and help him."

As Dol, Kritta, and Werril looked back at him blankly, there was a rustle from behind. Mordant Talliver was standing and looking at John grimly. Groaning inwardly, John turned to face him, preparing himself for a torrent of abuse.

Instead, Mordant said simply, "I'll do it. I'll go with you."

CHAPTER 13

"Are you serious?" John asked, almost choking on the words. He stared at the half-Gargon. Mordant Talliver was the last person he would have expected to volunteer for a life-saving mission.

A thought went through his mind: *Of course he's not serious, you fool. Any moment now he's going to start laughing at you.*

Mordant's face remained set in its grim expression. "Do I look like I'm joking?" he snapped. "There are sick people who need our help. What are you waiting for?"

"But . . . but . . . you —"

John did not have a chance to finish the sentence. At the end of the common room, a TravelTube door slid open, and an Examiner floated out.

"Emergency quarantine rule zero-zero-twelve. No further interaction between students is permitted," it droned. "All students confined to their dormitories until the flu epidemic has passed."

John glanced at Mordant. He was still unsure if the half-Gargon was trying to make a fool of him, but if they were both stuck in their dormitories, they would never get to the Zaleta Nebula.

There's no choice, I have to take the risk.

As the Examiner floated closer, John shouted, "NOW!"

Instantly, John, Mordant, and G-Vez dived through the open door of the TravelTube from which the Examiner had just exited.

John quickly looked back. Lights flashed across the Examiner's spherical head. Any moment a green force would paralyze them both.

He punched a panel on the inside of the TravelTube, hearing the Examiner's voice: "Rule zero-zero-eight-three . . ." as the door snapped shut.

"Deck three!" Mordant yelled.

The TravelTube hurtled straight down.

"No, we need to get to the main hangar, instead of deck three!" John shouted. "Computer —"

A tentacle slapped across his mouth before he could give the new order.

"The Examiners will be looking for us," hissed Mordant, "and they're hooked into the ship's systems. If we take the TravelTube to the hangar, that's where they'll start searching. Understand?"

John nodded. Mordant removed the tentacle and continued, "We'll have to do this fast. G-Vez, you set off an alarm to distract the Examiners. Got it?"

The silver droid bobbed at Mordant's shoulder and said, "Yes, Master Talliver. It will be my pleasure to assist you, sir."

Looking at John, Mordant said, "Running from deck three to the hangar should take about five minutes. When we get there, you find a nebula-diving pod. They'll be in the storage bay. I'll get us a ship."

"Can't we just be quick and grab the first one we see?"

Mordant rolled his eyes. "Use your brain," he said. "We need a ship with a docking system we can attach the pod to, and that can carry us a long way into the nebula. A nebula-diving pod can only last about thirty minutes in a core before beginning to degrade, so the closer we get, the better. By my calculations, the ship will have to withstand temperatures of more than two thousand degrees. Plus, Hyperspace High is in quarantine. We're surrounded by the Galactic Fleet. We need something super fast or we won't stand a chance of outrunning them."

John nodded. For the first time, it occurred to him that there might be some advantages to working alongside Mordant Talliver. Whatever else he might be, the half-Gargon was extremely intelligent: a walking encyclopedia of facts and figures.

"Which ship?" John asked.

"I don't know yet."

"Oh."

Mordant gave him a sharp look. "You just worry about the nebula-diver. I'll find us a ship," he said.

"Deck three." The TravelTube's doors opened. John stuck his head around the corner. Deck three housed more dormitories and additional cafeterias.

At the end of the corridor an Examiner passed, herding a group of students to their rooms.

"Get back," John whispered, pushing Mordant in the chest to stop him running out into the passage.

He peered around again. The Examiner had passed.

"Coast's clear!" he announced.

"Now!" said Mordant, pushing G-Vez out of the TravelTube, in the direction of the Examiners. As G-Vez drifted down the corridor, Mordant whispered, "Let's not hang around here," and dashed off toward the hangar deck.

John was surprised at how easy it was to get to the hangar deck unseen. Hyperspace High seemed almost completely deserted. He and Mordant had to stop once as some Meteor Medics passed, but they were obviously on their way to a new case of the flu and showed no interest in the two fugitives.

After dashing down emergency stairs and rarely-used corridors, the unlikely pair was soon standing outside a set of gigantic, heavily bolted double doors that led onto the main hangar.

"Locked!" John said, fuming. He bent over the electronic keypad. "I should have known. The ship's in quarantine. No craft is allowed to leave."

"It's not a problem," Mordant said, pushing past. To John's amazement, he tapped the keypad rapidly. Immediately, bolts slid back, and with a clank of metal, the doors opened.

"How on Earth did you do that?"

Mordant glanced back over his shoulder as he strode through the doors. "I have my ways."

"But that's a high-security code," John said. "How —"

"Just get the pod, John. I'll meet you in ship bay gamma." Mordant strode away in the direction of the ship bays, where Hyperspace High's spacecraft were kept when not in use.

Pausing to close the doors behind them, John raced away in the opposite direction.

Fortunately, with all access to the hangar deck sealed off, no one had bothered to lock the storage area. John opened it, pulling out his ThinScreen to double-check what he should actually be looking for. He had never seen a nebula-diving pod before.

Inside the storage area were Hyperspace High's smallest ships — star surfers, speed racers, and observation chambers, stacked neatly in rows.

John started searching the first row. He finally found what he was looking for at the end of the third.

The pod was a simple-looking machine. Resembling a large bullet made of shining silver, it was about ten feet long with small engines at the rear, stubby wings, a domed cockpit, and small suction holes for particle collection near its nose. The Hyperspace High logo was emblazoned across its shell in red letters.

From his quick ThinScreen cram session, John knew it was a fully independent craft able to operate in regions that would fry any normal ship. It carried almost no electronic circuits of any kind, just the most basic for communications and navigation, all of which were shielded to protect the vehicle from radiation. Even so, the heavily armored little craft could only protect him from the intense furnace heat of a nebula core for half an hour. After that, the heat inside would become too intense for his body to survive.

As quickly as he could, John found a robotic GravLifter and moved it under the pod. At the press of a button, the GravLifter's arms extended upward, grabbing the tiny craft with a clunk and moving it out of its storage compartment. John grabbed the GravLifter's towing handle and twisted. The heavy machine lifted off the floor on anti-grav pads, allowing him to easily pull it back toward the main hangar.

John found Mordant standing in the middle of ship bay gamma, arms and tentacles hugging his body, staring up at a spaceship John had never seen before.

Slightly bigger than private jets on Earth, it was sleekly beautiful. From a sharp nose, it flowed back in curves to sweeping wings fit with huge, powerful-looking engines. Flaming red, the ship looked as though someone had polished every inch of its surface. It gleamed under the hangar lights. There wasn't a single stray mark on it.

John whistled as he stopped beside Mordant. "Whoa. What is that?" he breathed.

Mordant's head turned. For a moment, he looked surprised to see John and a sneer crossed his face. Then he seemed to remember why he was in the hangar deck.

"Sergeant Jegger's Talios 720," Mordant said. "It's his pride and joy, and it costs a fortune. Beautiful, isn't it?"

John stared, his jaw dropping open. "Sergeant Jegger's private ship?" he said, gasping. "You have got to be kidding me, Mordant. We can't take that."

"It's the only ship I could find that can handle the temperature and has a dock. Jegger has the flu; he won't mind."

"But we'll definitely get expelled if we take it."

Mordant raised an eyebrow. "Whatever ship we take, we're probably going to be expelled," he answered. "Disobeying an Examiner, breaking into a sealed security area, stealing a spaceship, leaving Hyperspace High without permission . . . Do you want me to go on?"

"I get the point," John said dryly. He shrugged. "I'm pretty sure I flunked Hyperspace History anyway. Either way, I won't be coming back next semester."

"Any other day I'd be overjoyed," Mordant replied. "But it's looking like neither of us will be here next semester. Come on, let's get the nebula-diver docked."

When the pod had been attached to the docking mechanism, the two boys climbed up the steps of Sergeant Jegger's Talios 720.

Inside, the ship was as beautiful as it was on the outside: all deep, plush seats and shiny, new technology. Mordant handed John a flight suit and helmet.

"Should help protect us in the nebula," Mordant said, pulling a suit over his own uniform.

John changed quickly. The suit was bulky but felt light, and John found he could move easily in it. After pulling on boots and thick gloves, he fastened the helmet and walked to the cockpit. As he sat in the pilot's chair, an automatic harness strapped itself around his body. For a few moments, he forgot about Zhaldarian Flu as his gaze swept across the impressive control panel.

"This ship is awesome," he whispered.

"Yeah, and who said you were going to fly it?" said Mordant behind him.

Spinning the command chair around, John looked into the visor of Mordant's helmet. "As you are constantly pointing out to me," he said evenly, "I am pretty awful at Galactic Geography, but I'm a good pilot. It makes sense that you navigate while I do the flying."

Pointing out his own flaws seemed to convince Mordant. With a grunt, he dropped into the co-pilot's seat. "Get on with it, then," he snapped.

"Okay, preflight checks and taxi out into the main hangar." With confident expertise, John's fingers flicked over the controls. "Let's see what this machine can do."

The engines growled, sending a shudder through the Talios 720. With mounting excitement, John released the safety brakes, which allowed the ship to roll out of the ship bay and onto the main deck. "Ready for takeoff?" he asked, glancing at Mordant.

"Yup." The half-Gargon took over the

astrometric controls, bringing up star charts and plotting a course for the Zaleta Nebula.

"Darn." John pulled back on the controls quickly. The engine noise dropped.

"What? What's wrong?"

"We forgot about that."

Mordant's gaze followed John's finger. Ahead were the massive bay doors, and they were firmly closed. On the other side was space, but until the doors opened, the Talios was stuck on the hangar deck.

"Can we fly through those doors?" John asked.

"No way. They're solid mallux. You'll just wreck Jegger's ship, and there won't even be a scratch on the bay doors."

"So how do we get out of here?" John asked quietly.

Mordant was silent for a moment. "They'll only open with the highest-level security clearance. My code isn't going to get us out of here. It needs Jegger or the headmaster or the ship's computer —"

"I'll handle it," John said. He reached out and punched a button on the control screen.

"Zepp," he said loudly. "It's John. Can you hear me?"

"What are you doing?" whispered Mordant. "Stop! The ship's computer will never let us leave —"

John gestured at him to be silent.

"John," Zepp's voice said into John's helmet. "The Examiners are looking for you and Mordant Talliver. Why are you on Sergeant Jegger's private ship?"

"Zepp," said John. "I need the biggest favor

I've ever asked of you. I need you to open the bay doors of the main hangar deck."

Silence.

"You do not have the authority to make that request," the computer said after a few moments.

"That's why I asked it as a favor," John said urgently. "Please, Zepp. Mordant and I are going to the Zaleta Nebula. There might be a cure for Zhaldarian Flu there. We'll never get permission to leave the ship — you have to help us."

"As the ship's computer, I have to follow the rules, John," Zepp said. "You do not have the authority —"

"I know I don't have the authority, Zepp," John cut in, the desperation in his voice rising. "What I do have is a friend who could open the bay doors for me. Almost everyone on board Hyperspace High has the flu. Some of them aren't going to make it. But if we're successful, they'll live. All of them."

"It will be too dangerous. You might not survive."

"Listen, Zepp. I know you are programmed to keep the students on board Hyperspace High from harm at all costs. There is a risk for me and Mordant, but surely that risk is outweighed by the possibility that hundreds, perhaps thousands, of lives will be saved if we're successful."

Another silence stretched out. Seconds passed.

Come on, Zepp, John thought furiously. *Come on, come on, come on . . .*

Finally, the computer spoke. "You are correct. My source code forbids me to harm students," Zepp said. "If opening the doors will prevent suffering, then my program must execute your request."

As John watched, the giant bay doors began to slide open, slowly revealing the stars beyond.

"Good luck, John," Zepp said as the Talios's engines roared into life again. "You, too, Mordant. Be careful."

CHAPTER 14

Its jets burning, the Talios 720 blasted through the bay doors and into space.

Feeling raw power thrumming through the ship, John moved the control stick, intending to steer away from the massive shape of Hyperspace High.

Instead, the Talios spun crazily.

"What are you doing?" yelled Mordant as they whirled.

John jerked back the control stick, straightening out the craft. Pressing the power panel, he sent the ship soaring into space.

"Sorry," he muttered. "These controls are way more sensitive than a t-dart's controls are, I guess."

"I knew I should have insisted on flying," Mordant said.

John bit back a snotty response. "Which way?" he asked instead.

"I'm plotting a course now," Mordant replied in a businesslike tone. "Take a heading zero-eight-six-three-nine into the Omega Region. There are a few obstructions, but nothing serious, and then I can give you an almost direct path. For the next few light-years there's nothing but clear black space, so you'll be able to kick up the speed."

"Got it," replied John. With a glance at the astrometrics screen, he carefully pulled the Talios around onto a new course and powered up the hyperspace drive.

"Uh-oh," Mordant said. "Looks like we've got company. Galactic Fleet."

"Let's see if we can outrun them. Jumping to hyperspace on my mark. In three . . . two . . . one . . . mark."

"Oh . . . my . . . whoaaaa!" John yelped, as the Talios leaped forward like a missile. Any jump to hyperspace meant a huge surge of energy and speed, but Sergeant Jegger's ship was beyond anything John had ever experienced. With a deep, throaty roar, the engines flung the Talios forward at a speed that pressed John back in the pilot's seat, as he struggled to keep the control stick steady.

"I have got to get my dad to buy me one of these," Mordant murmured.

Inside his helmet, John raised his eyebrows. Over the summer vacation John's dad had bought him a new skateboard. *And he made me do a ton of weeding to get it,* he thought.

The half-Gargon boy interrupted his thoughts. "Trouble: those ships jumped with us. They're still on our tail."

Before he'd even finished speaking, the communications system crackled.

"This is Captain Lassco of the Galactic Fleet," a voice boomed in John's ear. "Pilot of the Talios 720 out of Hyperspace High, identify yourself."

"Rats," John muttered.

"Repeat: ship out of Hyperspace High, identify yourself."

John flipped a switch to open the channel. "John Riley," he said, trying to sound more confident than he felt. "A student from Hyperspace High. We're just —"

"All traffic to and from Hyperspace High is suspended by order of the Galactic Council," said Captain Lassco, interrupting. "It's a quarantine zone. Turn your ship around and return to Hyperspace High immediately, John Riley."

"Sorry, captain, no can do," John said. "We're on our way to find a cure for Zhaldarian Flu."

"You do not have clearance for your mission," the captain said insistently. "Turn your ship around."

John cut the communications.

Turning to Mordant, he quickly asked, "Can we outrun them?"

Mordant shrugged. "They're flying Blaze-Class Fighters. Very, very fast. They'll match our speed. Plus, they're Galactic Fleet-trained pilots."

Without hesitation, John flicked the communications switch again. "Negative, Captain Lassco," he said. "We're not turning around. We're trying to save lives here."

"They're almost on us," said Mordant, panic creeping into his voice.

"This is your last warning, John Riley," said Lassco. "Turn your ship around and return to Hyperspace High, or I will be forced to open fire. The Galactic Council will not risk the flu spreading. Billions of lives are at stake."

"There's no chance of infection. We're going —"

"Don't tell them where we're going," hissed Mordant. "We'll never get rid of them."

"We're not going anywhere near any inhabited planets," John continued. "Call off your ships."

Out of the corner of his eye, John saw two streaks stream past the port side of the Talios — both streaks John recognized as X-11 missiles. In a massive burst, they exploded in front of the Talios.

"That was a warning shot, John Riley. Turn your ship around."

John's fingers swiftly moved across the power controls.

"Sorry, Captain Lassco, I just can't do that," he said, as he pulled the Talios into an accelerating swoop away from the following Blaze-Class Fighters.

"They're following . . . weapons fire!" Mordant yelled.

John jerked the control stick. The Talios rolled, as two more X-11 missiles exploded close by.

"Give me a new heading," he said through gritted teeth. His hand reached out again, pushing the ship to maximum speed while he guided it into a complex maneuver of evasive twists and rolls.

Another close explosion shook the ship from side to side.

"Where to?" Mordant yelled.

"Anywhere I can shake them off."

Mordant leaned over his control panel, his fingers a blur as he scanned star charts. "There's an asteroid field at heading two-nine-eight-three-four."

John was already pushing the control stick. Its engines screaming, the Talios swerved away. From the corner of his eye, John saw two blips on the sensor screen immediately turn to follow them.

"Incoming!" shouted Mordant.

The Talios spun as more missiles streaked past. John fought for control as they detonated, rocking the ship.

"The pilots are too good!" Mordant yelled. "You're not going to lose them."

Ignoring him, John shouted, "How far to the asteroid field?'

Mordant swung back to his screens. "A million miles away and closing fast. Slow down, John."

"No!" shouted John.

"You can't go through an asteroid field at hyperspace speed," Mordant shouted, shocked. "It's suicidal!"

"It's the only way to get them off our tail!" John shouted back. "Hold on."

"You won't even be able to see . . . gaaaaah!" Wrapping his tentacles around his head, Mordant ducked down in his seat.

Unblinking, John stared ahead, moving the control stick with lightning-fast reflexes. Darting and rolling, the spaceship skimmed past a blur of giant whirling boulders of ice and rock.

"Mordant, we're through!" he yelled seconds later. "Did they slow down? Are we clear of them?"

Still making choking noises, Mordant unwrapped his tentacles from his head and leaned over the screen. He gasped. "No. They came through at the same speed as you . . . You're all insane."

John cursed.

"They're charging antimatter blasters!" shrieked Mordant.

With a sinking feeling in his stomach, John whipped the control stick around again. A terrifying bolt of dark purple light sped past and disappeared into space.

"Charging again. Oh no, they've locked onto us. They're going to destroy us. We're going to d—"

"Captain Lassco, we surrender!" John shouted, slowing the Talios.

"They're powering down weapons," Mordant babbled. "I thought we were dead . . ." But his last few words were gibberish to John.

The ship's computer didn't translate Gargon swearing.

The communications channel crackled. "Excellent choice," the Galactic Fleet captain said dryly. "Turn your ship around and prepare to —"

"No! I demand to speak to Councillor Tarz," John cut in. "Immediately."

CHAPTER 15

"Listen, son," said the captain, sounding angry. "You've just broken a Galactic Council quarantine order. You're in no position to make demands."

John clenched his fists, knowing the mission depended on convincing Councillor Tarz to let him and Mordant go. He'd met Emmie's dad at the Space Spectacular, and was sure he could convince him.

"We're trying to save lives, Captain Lassco," John insisted. "Please. Let me speak to the councillor."

"Turn your ship around and return to Hyperspace High," Captain Lassco said. "I don't want to fire on you again." From the tone in the captain's voice, John knew this was his final word.

The communications channel crackled again. "I'll speak to him," said a new voice. "This is Councillor Tarz. What do you want, John?"

"Councillor Tarz," John said quickly. "You have to let us proceed."

"Our orders come straight from the Galactic President," said Emmie's father. "No ship is to approach or depart from Hyperspace High. Even if I wanted to let you go, John, it's out of my hands."

"I understand, Councillor." John hesitated for a second, wondering whether to reveal his plan. *It's Emmie's dad*, he reminded himself. "But there are microbes at the core of the Zaleta Nebula," he continued. "The headmaster thinks they might be a cure."

"The headmaster has also told the council this," Emmie's father said. "The information is under consideration."

"And while the council considers, my friends are dying," said John, with urgency. "Think of Emmie."

"How is she? Is there any change in her condition?" asked Councillor Tarz. John heard the worry and fear beneath his calm tone.

"I saw her a couple of hours ago. She's very sick, Councillor. Our friend Kaal will die soon. Please let me try to help them. You'll never forgive yourself if you don't."

For a few moments, the Sillaran councillor didn't reply. Then slowly, he said, "You know I think highly of you, John. You're a good friend to Emmie, and I believe you can complete this mission, but there are procedures we must follow."

"With respect, sir, that's not good enough," John replied, trying his best to sound reasonable. "This is the only hope we have."

Again, the councillor was silent. Seconds ticked by.

"You don't intend to land on any planet? There's no risk that you could spread the infection?" he asked eventually.

"No, sir. We — Mordant Talliver and I — we're going to collect the microbes and fly straight back again."

"I see," Councillor Tarz said quietly. "It is a dangerous scheme. The core of a nebula is not a hospitable place."

"Sir," Captain Lassco's voice interrupted the councillor. "You cannot even be thinking about this. The president —"

"The president is not in command of this fleet, Captain Lassco," said Councillor Tarz coldly. "I am."

"But, sir —"

Councillor Tarz did not allow him to finish. "The Galactic President has said that no ship is to leave Hyperspace High," he said quickly. "I hereby invoke Galactic Emergency protocol sixteen A to overturn that order. John, you may proceed."

"Councillor Tarz, I must protest," spluttered the captain.

"Your protest is noted, Lassco. Return to quarantine guard."

"Aye aye, turning back."

As John watched, the two blips on the scanner screen moved back in the direction of Hyperspace High. "Thank you, sir," John said quietly.

"Leave now, John. By invoking protocol sixteen A, I have just declared the Galactic President unfit to lead and assumed command. I will be sacked within a few hours. It would be best if you had returned to Hyperspace High with the microbes by then."

"I'll do my best."

Councillor Tarz's reply cracked with emotion. "If you save Emmie, John, I will never be able to repay you. Now, go."

                              * * *

"We're approaching the Zaleta Nebula," said Mordant an hour later.

"I see it," John replied. Ahead was a great cloud of pinks, purples, and blues, shimmering with the light of newborn stars. "Dropping speed to hyperspace factor one-fifty."

The Talios swept into the nebula. "How far to the core?" asked John.

Mordant pored over his charts. "About five light-years, heading two-two-six-two-eight. But be careful, I'm already getting system interference."

John looked around as he turned the ship to follow the new course heading. It wasn't the first time he had been inside a nebula, but he would still never get used to the sight. Around him, suns burned among the delicate swirling clouds, orbited by spheres of denser gases and great balls of rock that might one day become planets. Directly ahead was the nebula's glowing core.

"Temperature rising," said Mordant. "Five hundred degrees plus."

Smoothly guiding the ship past rocky space debris, John held the course. The glowing core grew larger in the middle of the viewing screen.

"A thousand degrees and rising."

John nodded. He could feel the heat seeping through the hull of the Talios. Even beneath the flight suit and quarantine suit, his skin was beginning to prickle.

"One thousand five hundred degrees. Keep her steady."

The core of the nebula now filled the viewing

window. The visor of John's helmet darkened automatically to protect his eyes from the glare.

"One thousand eight hundred degrees," said Mordant calmly. "And we are stopping in ten seconds."

John pulled the control stick. The Talios skimmed past a comet.

"In five . . . four . . . three . . . two . . . one. Two thousand degrees."

"Dropping out of hyperspeed," said John. The Talios shrieked as jets came on line, rapidly reducing the ship's speed until it came to a complete stop.

"At this temperature, the ship's systems are going to start degrading in about thirty-five minutes," said Mordant.

"That's about the same length of time that the nebula-diver can withstand core temperatures," said John, unclipping his harness and pulling off his helmet. "Let's get to it."

In the Talios's small airlock, Mordant flipped open the hatch to the ship's dock. Beneath was the interior of the nebula-diver.

John peered into a small, dark space, which was just big enough for a single person to fit through. If that.

"Looks like a squeeze," he said under his breath. "Hope I fit."

Mordant's head snapped up in surprise. "Who cares whether you fit," he said. "I'm going."

"Um, no. I don't think so," John replied quickly. "I already checked, and my body should be able to withstand the environment, for a while at least. But it might not be safe for Gargons."

"Tough," replied Mordant. "I'm going, and that's all there is to it."

John groaned inwardly. This was not the time for Mordant Talliver to start behaving like his old self, and John realized he still didn't trust him.

Mordant might be intelligent, but John had seen him under pressure before and knew he might crack if he ran into difficulties.

John took a deep breath. "Look, Mordant," he said, trying to sound calm. "We've worked pretty well together so far, let's not start fighting now."

He stepped toward the hatch.

"No, let's start," replied Mordant, putting a tentacle on John's chest and pushing him back. "You're not in command here. And you've never used a nebula-diver before."

"Have *you*?"

"No," Mordant admitted, "but I've studied them."

Frustration building, John slapped away the tentacle. "We don't have time for this."

"Just let me go, then."

John squeezed his eyes shut, forcing himself to remain cool. "Star, gas, laser?" he suggested, as he opened them again.

The half-Gargon hesitated, then dropped his tentacle. "Yeah, all right. Best of three."

Dropping to their knees, the two students beat their fists on the surface of the pod. "One . . . two . . . three."

"Star," said Mordant, holding up a hand, fingers spread.

"Gas." John showed a clenched fist.

"Stars burn gas. That's one point to me."

"Go."

"One . . . two . . . three . . . laser," said Mordant, pointing two fingers at John.

John held up his fist again. "Gas clogs laser. One point to me."

Mordant scowled. "One . . . two . . . three . . . gas."

"Star," said John, lifting his hand. "Bad luck."

Swearing under his breath, Mordant stepped back.

With beads of sweat running down his forehead, John stepped through the hatch, kneeling inside the nebula-diver and reaching for the controls.

They were the most basic he had seen on any spacecraft: what looked like small motorcycle handlebars for steering, with a throttle for power, an ignition button, and a lever for the braking jets. Strapped alongside the tiny pilot space were six pressurized canisters. The small navigation panel and a microphone were the only signs of electronics.

"Ready?" said the half-Gargon as John lay down, his hands gripping the steering unit.

"Ready," said John.

"Be back here in half an hour. If you're down there any longer than that the radiation will kill you for sure."

"Thanks for reminding me," replied John. "Glad to hear you care."

"Yeah . . . well . . . good luck, I suppose," Mordant said.

"And to you —"

The hatch slammed shut.

John wiggled into the space. It was dark, and there was barely room to move. With one hand, he powered up the navigation screen.

Through a speaker by his head, John heard Mordant's voice: "Disengaging dock."

For a second John held his breath, trying to calm the rising fear.

Part of his brain was raving that it was madness to fly into the burning heart of a nebula in such a tiny craft.

But it was quickly followed by an image of Kaal lying in his hospital bed, skin sagging and changing color.

Letting out his breath in a hiss, John stabbed at the ignition button.

With a blast of rocket boosters, the nebula-diver moved away from the underside of the Talios.

John felt his stomach lurch. Through the small viewing window, he could see the fierce glow of the nebula's core.

Gritting his teeth, he headed toward the heat and radiation. There was no turning back now.

CHAPTER 16

John twisted the throttle, sending the nebula-diver rocketing toward the nebula's core. Immediately, a swirling blast of gas caught the tiny, bullet-shaped craft, blowing it off course. Pulling the steering control this way and that, John struggled to regain control.

It wasn't easy. Flying the pod was nothing like piloting a normal spacecraft. The little machine felt as light as a feather and was totally at the mercy of the flurries of gas outside. And the heat was rising steeply, too.

John's fingers felt slippery, and sweat ran quickly down his forehead as he fought to steer the pod.

"Automatic temperature controls engaged," said an electronic voice in his ear. Immediately, John began to feel somewhat cooler, and he realized that the flight suit he was wearing had inbuilt technology that adjusted to keep him comfortable in all environments.

John glanced at the navigation screen, which Mordant had remote programmed from the Talios. It showed a thirty-minute countdown and a flashing light marked the meeting point. John didn't need help finding the core; its glare filled the pod's small viewing window.

Suddenly, another gust of hot gas sent the

craft tumbling back the way it had come. Giving the jets more thrust, John swerved crazily through the thick mist.

Through the viewing screen, he caught a glimpse of Mordant Talliver in the pilot's seat of the Talios, a smug look on his face as he touched the control panels.

Mordant's arrogant look brought back a flood of memories. All the times the black-tentacled boy had schemed to get John into trouble hit him at once. As the pod surged back toward the nebula's core, he felt a rising surge of panic, realizing that his survival depended solely on Mordant Talliver, who — only two weeks earlier — had tried to turn Emmie against him and sabotaged deadly Defendroid robots that might have killed him and Kaal at the Space Spectacular show.

In his haste to get to the Zaleta Nebula, John

hadn't stopped to dwell on why Mordant had volunteered to come along. Now, it was quickly dawning on him how strangely the half-Gargon boy was behaving. Of all people, why would Mordant Talliver offer to join him on a life-threatening mission?

What possible reason would he have?

He's trying to get rid of me.

"You're doing okay, John," said Mordant's voice through a speaker by John's head. "Follow your current heading. See you in twenty-nine minutes."

An icy chill crept down John's spine. Would Mordant be there when he got back? It would be easy for him to fly back to Hyperspace High, claiming that John had never returned from the nebula's core. No one would ever be able to prove otherwise.

No, he wanted to take the pod himself, John

reminded himself. *He would have trusted me to stay for him. I have to trust him.*

Pushing his fears to the back of his mind, John jerked the throttle. The tiny pod roared forward.

Another squall of gas hit, threatening to throw him off course once more. John wrenched the steering control around, breathing heavily and feeling more claustrophobic within the narrow space with every passing second. *It's like cyber jousting,* he told himself. *Just find the balance and trust yourself.* Remembering the way that Emmie stayed on top of a ball with perfect poise, John turned the ship slightly, trying to ride the wind instead of battling against it.

It worked. The nebula-diver was still buffeted by streaming hot gases, but now it was traveling faster and staying on course.

"Flight suit control systems degrading," said

the electronic voice in his ear. "Twenty minutes to failure."

John glanced at the navigation screen. Twenty-three minutes before he had to get back. For the last three of those minutes, the flight suit would offer no protection at all. Only the hull of the pod itself would protect him from the deadly heat and radiation. He twisted the throttle again, wringing every last ounce of speed from the little machine. Minutes passed. By now, the gas outside John's viewing screen had become so dense that John could see nothing but a bright glare. The winds dropped, making flying easier. A readout on the navigation display told him that the temperature outside was now over 5,000 degrees Celsius, as hot as the surface of the sun.

Seventeen minutes left.

His forehead lined in concentration, John

sent the nebula-diver skimming onward. He could feel the heat building again, as the flight suit's systems began to collapse.

How will I know when to collect the microbes?

John gulped as the thought hit him. He glanced at the navigation panel. In less than two minutes he would have used up half of his time. If there was any chance of making it back to the Talios safely, he would have to start his return journey soon. He had to get the microbes and start heading back.

But if I'm not at the core, I'll just be going back with canisters full of useless gas.

A memory stirred. John was sitting in front of a ThinScreen in Hyperspace High's library with Emmie, studying for Galactic Geography. Zepp had been speaking while they both scribbled notes. In his head, John could hear Zepp's voice: "The core of a nebula is surrounded by turbulent gas but, within the core itself, there is a steady gravitational force."

John eased off the throttle. The tiny pod continued to slip through the dense gas smoothly. The wind outside had dropped to nothing.

I'm already inside the core.

John quickly fired braking jets, bringing the pod to a stop. He reached for the lever that would fill the empty canisters with the core's precious gas microbes. Gripping the lever, he pushed.

Nothing happened.

John's hands scrambled across the tiny control panel flicking whatever switches they touched. Still nothing.

Grasping the suction lever again, he pulled it. This time, a steady whirring sound began behind him. John wriggled, trying to create enough room to see over his shoulder. The six clear canisters were filling up quickly. Within each was a pale blue mist, tiny microbes sparking like miniscule suns. The mist became more and more dense until a buzz sounded, and a green light switched to red on the panel in front of him.

Full.

Get me out of here.

"Flight suit failure in fourteen minutes."

With a shock, John realized he was panting. The pod was like an oven, and his skin was slick with sweat. Pushing the lever back to its original position, he sealed the canisters. With a last glance over his shoulder at the twinkling tubes of gas, he muttered, "You'd better work," and curled his fingers around the throttle. A second later, the nebula-diver swept around, and began heading back the way it had come.

As the tiny diver made its way away from

the core, John could feel the temperature rising sharply.

"Flight suit failure in eight minutes."

"Come on!" John yelled. He gasped to take a breath of the hot air. Beads of sweat trickled into his eyes, but there was nothing he could do about them. Blinking, he silently urged the pod onward, keeping the throttle open to maximum, and glanced at the small navigation panel. He was less than a third of the way back to the meeting point. He twisted the steering control as a gust of gas hurled the pod sideways.

"Flight suit failure in five minutes."

The heat was intense now, the river of sweat pouring into John's eyes almost blinding. Gasping hot lungfuls of air, he blinked, searching through the swirling mist for the shining-red Talios, even though he knew he was still too far away.

Hang in there, John, he thought. *Only a*

few minutes to go, and then you'll be flying back to Hyperspace High with the microbes that will cure Kaal and Emmie.

"Flight suit failure in one minute."

By now, the suit's systems were functioning at a bare minimum, and John knew he would soon be roasted alive by the heat radiating from the nebula. He tightened his grip on the throttle and steered the nebula-diver away from the core.

"Please be there, Mordant. Please be there," John repeated over and over to himself as he wrestled the tiny pod against external forces, bringing it closer and closer to the point he was to meet the half-Gargon.

He glanced at the time. The swirling gases were thinning now. John peered ahead, shaking his head to try to clear his sight. The navigation panel flashed. He had made it to the meeting point.

A groan escaped John's mouth. The Talios 720 was nowhere to be seen.

CHAPTER 17

"Mordant. Come in, Mordant. Can you hear me?" John yelled into the microphone next to his head. The only response was the crackle of static.

Through clouds of gas, John could see stars blinking, but there was no sign of the Talios 720 anywhere.

Firing jets to spin the craft, he looked in every direction.

Nothing.

He was alone.

John tried the communications once more, an edge of desperation in his voice now. "Come on, answer for crying out loud. Stop this, Mordant. You can't just leave me here."

A steady hiss was all he heard.

John smashed a fist into the control panel. "I guess I was right about you after all, Mordant," he spat bitterly. "I should have listened to my instincts."

"Flight suit system failure," said the electronic voice.

John sucked in a lungful of hot air. Already the heat was almost unbearable, and he had no extra protection now. Soon radiation from the nebula's core would overwhelm the pod. At the same time, the core's gravity would pull the pod back toward it.

Long before any rescuers arrived — assuming any even did — the pod (and John) would be utterly destroyed.

The microbes will never make it back to Hyperspace High, he thought. *Kaal will die . . . maybe Emmie, too, and hundreds of others.*

Knowing it was useless, he jabbed a finger at the communications system again, switching to all the emergency channels Sergeant Jegger had taught him.

"Distress call level one. Repeat: distress call level one. All ships. Nebula-diver stranded at the core of the Zaleta Nebula. Coordinates two-two-six-three-seven. Distress call level one."

At the same time, he twisted the throttle

again, surging the pod forward. Blinking sweat out of his eyes, John powered away from the glowing core.

There wasn't enough fuel in the pod to get back to Hyperspace High, or even to escape the nebula, but if he could get further from the core, at least it would take longer to be sucked back in. Further away it would be slightly cooler, too. Maybe the extra time it gave him might be long enough for a passing ship to hear his message and rescue him.

Yeah, right, John thought, shaking his head sadly. The chances of a ship close enough to even hear his message were minute.

As the pod moved through the nebula on wings of roaring gas, John felt unexpectedly calm, as if his mind had become detached from the heat and the thirst and the terror.

Instead, he looked around him, marveling at the sight of the Zaleta Nebula. Whatever fate awaited him, he was light-years from Earth, seeing wonders no human being had ever dreamed of.

It's not such a bad way to die, John thought. *I just wish they knew on Hyperspace High that I did my best for them.*

With a sigh, John watched glimmering tangles of gas in which stars were being born, wondering if Lorem would find a way to tell his parents what had happened to him.

A spark of light caught his attention. *A new sun?* he wondered, as he struggled to absorb what was happening around him.

Seconds later, the spark turned into the roaring engines of a Talios 720. John hardly recognized it as the same ship that he had left half an hour earlier. Its shining red hull was covered in dents, scratches, and deep scars. Nevertheless, the engines were working, and that was really the only thing John cared about at all.

He managed to let out a small cheer as the ship maneuvered above him. A loud clunk signaled that the docking system had locked on. The hatch clanked open.

"Did you get the microbes?" demanded Mordant, before falling back, coughing, as a blast of hot air rose from the nebula-diver. "Whoa, you still alive in there?"

"Water." John coughed as he rose from the hatch in a cloud of steam and collapsed into the co-pilot's seat. "Give me water."

Mordant yanked open a locker and handed him a bottle. John twisted the top off, pouring a stream down his throat and over his face. A few seconds later, he looked at the half-Gargon sharply.

"Where have you been?" John said. "You were supposed to wait for me. I could have died."

Mordant shrugged. "And you would have died if it hadn't been for me."

"What are you talking about?" John asked, frowning.

"While I was waiting, a meteor came out of nowhere," Mordant explained. "Pulled in by the nebula core's gravity, I guess. Anyway, the ship's computer calculated it was on a collision course with you."

John wiped water and sweat from his eyes. "I didn't see any meteor," he said.

"Of course you didn't," Mordant said,

rolling his eyes. "That's because I managed to change its trajectory."

"You did what?" John cried. "But there aren't any weapons on this ship. How did you make it change course?"

"With the ship," said Mordant. "Didn't you notice it's a little banged up?"

John's eyes widened in surprise. "Let me get this straight," he blurted. "You crashed Sergeant Jegger's ship into a meteor on purpose to make sure it wouldn't hit me?"

"Yes. I would have told you I was going to be late, but the communications system kind of got smashed."

"You did that to save me?" John stared at Mordant Talliver, his jaw hanging open. "Wow. Thanks."

Mordant scowled. "No, idiot. I did it to save

the mission. Speaking of which, let's get out of here. You got the microbes, right?"

John nodded, happy to let the half-Gargon fly them back to Hyperspace High.

"Ready?" asked Mordant, glancing over at him.

The safety harness closed around John. "Ready," he said.

CHAPTER 18

An hour later, John was leaning forward over the scanner. "We've picked up a tail," he said. "Two ships off our port and starboard bows. Maintaining their distance."

"Probably Captain whatshisname — Lassco — again," Mordant replied calmly. "Giving us an escort back for the last lap. Not much use now. Those antimatter blasters would have been helpful with that meteor earlier, though."

"I guess they had to keep the quarantine perimeter in place," John replied. "Besides, we got through okay."

"All that's left is to land this thing and hope the headmaster was right about those microbes," Mordant said, nodding at the viewing screen. Ahead was the vast, white shape of Hyperspace High, lights blazing at every viewing window.

"Will you be okay to bring her in?" John asked.

He got a withering look in return. "Do I look like I need your help?"

After all they'd been through, John decided to let it pass.

As Mordant sent the Talios diving toward the ship, the main hangar doors opened. A few seconds later, the ship settled onto the deck. Behind them the bay doors slid back into place. With a roaring sound that lasted a few seconds, the hangar was flooded with oxygen.

Not waiting to change out of his flight suit, John yanked open the hatch to the nebula-diving pod and its precious cargo.

* * *

Mordant and John stepped down carefully from the battered Talios, each cradling three of the nebula-diver's canisters.

A door opened. Two Examiners appeared from a TravelTube and glided toward the boys at top speed.

"Students John Riley and Mordant Talliver, you have broken sixteen level-one school rules and eight level-two school rules. Proceed to the detention center and prepare to be expelled."

"Sorry," said John, continuing ahead. "We're busy right now."

"Rule zero-zero-eight-three: Examiners are to be obeyed at all times. Failure to comply will ensure more severe punishment."

"More severe?" said Mordant, walking alongside John. "How much more severe are we talking? When you expel us, are you going to call us names, too?"

"Proceed to airlock BZ. Comply within three seconds." Lights began to flash across the Examiners' heads as they prepared to use their paralyzing force fields.

"Zepp!" called John quickly. "Can you help us out here?"

The Examiners' lights faded. "Rule siiixtwooo . . ." the first robot droned, its voice slowing. A second later, both robots dropped to the floor, their egg-shaped bodies rolling lifelessly.

"I've always wanted to do that," said Zepp's voice, sounding cheerful. "The Examiners are supposed to be untouchable. No one has ever turned them off before."

"You're the best, Zepp," said John. "Could you —"

". . . make sure you don't meet any more between here and the medical wing?" said the computer, anticipating the rest of John's question. "I'm sure I can divert the rest of them."

"Medical wing," the TravelTube announced a few moments later. John and Mordant raced through the doors before they had fully opened.

"Dr. Kasaria!" John shouted, as they sprinted into the reception area. "We've got a cure!"

John skidded to a halt, Mordant close behind him, as they both looked around in shock. The situation had deteriorated even further while they had been away.

Dr. Kasaria was taking notes at her desk. Her forehead was slick with sweat, her metallic-looking skin was glowing, her black eyes were glazed and weary-looking.

She's getting sick, John thought.

Through the screen into the quarantine ward, he could see Meteor Medics hurrying between beds of screaming patients.

Straightening up, Dr. Kasaria glared at the two boys. "What do you want now, John Riley?" she snapped. "Kaal's condition has not improved. As you can see, no one's condition has improved."

"This might help," John said softly, holding up a tube of sparkling blue gas for the doctor to see.

Whatever reaction John had been expecting, it certainly wasn't a scowl. "Out of all the thousands of staff and students on Hyperspace High, only ninety-six do not have Zhaldarian Flu," Dr. Kasaria said firmly. "Several of my patients are not expected to make it through the night."

She paused for a second, fixing John and Mordant with an icy look. "And you two are playing games with me."

"We're not playing games," replied John urgently. "I promise. You see, these canisters contain microbes from the center of the Zaleta Nebula. The headmaster said there were some scientists who believed this could cure Zhaldraian Flu."

"What scientists? What were they called?" the doctor barked, rising from her chair. Was the doctor just worried and overtired, wondered John, or was her angry reaction an early symptom of the sickness?

"I . . . uh . . . don't know their names."

"That's because there are no such scientists!" Dr. Kasaria shrieked. "Anyone who had found a cure for Zhaldarian Flu would be among the most famous scientists in the universe. Yet you don't know their names, and neither do I!"

"But —"

"No buts, John Riley," the doctor spat, pounding her fist on the desk. "There is no cure for Zhaldarian Flu. Now stop wasting my time, and leave before I call an Examiner."

"Come on, John, let's get out of here," hissed Mordant, pulling at John's elbow.

"No, Mordant. We have to —"

"Just come," hissed the half-Gargon. Something in his tone forced John to turn.

"We've got to get the microbes to the patients," said John desperately, as Mordant dragged him into the corridor.

"Yes, but we're not going to do it getting hauled off by Examiners!" Mordant shot back. "Come on. We'll have to find some other way in."

John glanced up into Mordant's eyes. "Have you got a plan?"

Slowly, Mordant nodded. "We need a distraction," he said.

"What distraction is going to keep Dr. Kasaria from her patients?" John replied.

"The only one she won't be able to resist," said Mordant, handing John the canisters.

*　*　*

"Dr. Kasaria, it's Mordant. He's sick!" John yelled, as he helped the half-Gargon back through the door of the medical wing. "We made it as far as the Center and he suddenly collapsed."

"Oh, no, I feel terrible all of a sudden," Mordant groaned. "I must be coming down with something."

The doctor eyed them both warily. "Is this another of your games, John Riley?"

John shook his head. "No, he just dropped. I don't know what's wrong with him."

"But Mordant is immune to Zhaldarian Flu." Lines appeared across Dr. Kasaria's forehead. "I checked myself."

"It's not Zhaldarian Flu. He started groaning

in pain and wrapping his tentacles around his stomach," John said. "We've been to the Zaleta Nebula, so maybe he picked up something there."

"Help!" moaned Mordant in a voice of pure agony. He slipped to his knees, eyes rolling back in his head as he fell sideways, crashing into a cart loaded with medical equipment. His hand reached out as if to find support. Grabbing at the cart, Mordant brought it crashing down on top of himself.

"Meteor Medics!" shouted Dr. Kasaria, leaping across the room. "Get out of the way, John."

Those were exactly the words John had been hoping to hear.

"Yes, Dr. Kasaria," John said, stumbling backward. His hand reached out, searching for the panel he knew was there. Silently, a door slipped open.

While the doctor knelt by Mordant's head, straining to lift the cart off his body, John stepped back. Closing the door again quickly, he sprinted to the end of the hallway and into the room where he had last seen Kaal.

The room was empty apart from his friend's bed. John breathed a quick sigh of relief. The Meteor Medic that had been there earlier had obviously been reassigned to a new emergency. Most of the machines and monitors around him had been switched off.

Then a horrible thought struck him.

Does Dr. Kasaria expect Kaal to die tonight?

John's knees almost buckled when he looked down on his friend, knowing his guess was correct.

Kaal's body had wasted further in the few hours since John had last seen him. His skin had stopped changing color, but patches of what appeared to be a colored fungus were growing all over him. His withered body thrashed, and he moaned constantly.

"Kaal, can you hear me?"

No response. The Derrilian's eyes remained closed. Even in his weakened state, his huge body strained against the straps that held him down.

John felt terror well up in his stomach. *What if the cure doesn't work? What if I'm too late? What if . . .*

"Get a grip, John. It has to work," he hissed under his breath. John looked around and spotted an oxygen mask on a cart in the corner of the room. Snatching it up, he fixed a nearby tube to the canister of gas and fed the tube into the mask. Leaning over Kaal, he pressed the mask to his friend's face.

"That's right, buddy, breathe it in," he whispered as he watched the Derrilian's chest rise and fall.

A few seconds later, Kaal stopped straining against the straps. With a drawn-out sigh, he collapsed against the bed.

Closing off the gas flow to the mask, John hesitated.

He didn't want to leave Kaal's side, but there were hundreds of other sufferers. Knowing Mordant could only keep Dr. Kasaria busy for so long, John ran to the next room.

By the time he returned to the reception area, Mordant seemed to be having a fit. *Turns out acting is another thing Mordant's good at,* thought

John. Mordant's performance was worthy of an Oscar.

Dr. Kasaria and the Meteor Medics were trying to scan him, but his arms and tentacles kept whipping away the medical instruments, sending them smashing against walls.

Holding his breath, John crept past, stepping through the disinfectant field and into the quarantine ward.

Here, the volume was almost deafening. Patients cursed and screamed at him and at each other, throwing themselves against their straps as they tried to attack anything.

Keeping low, John raced past Doctor Graal. Her tentacles were waving around in the air crazily, while what John guessed was a stream of Gargon curses screeched out from her drooling mouth.

Only a handful of the flu victims had progressed beyond the violent stage of the disease and were lying quietly, and Emmie was among them.

Tears pricked John's eyes as he reached her. His friend's normally golden skin was blotchy and sludge green, her blue eyes were bloodshot and staring blankly at the ceiling.

With a heightened sense of urgency, John ducked down beside her bed and pushed the oxygen mask to her face. Allowing her to take several lungfuls, and hoping it was enough, he hurried over to the next bed.

Through the screen he could see Dr. Kasaria standing, her face like thunder. Mordant was also rising.

Realizing there was no time to dose every patient individually, John looked around the room frantically, trying to find a faster way to administer the gas.

In one corner of the room stood a large oxygen tank. His eyes followed the tube that extended from it, and he realized that it was feeding oxygen to every patient on the ward through their face masks.

He quickly detached the tube and reconnected it to the canister. As he watched, a glowing blue gas passed through the clear tubes and slowly, gently made its way into every oxygen mask.

"How dare you pretend you're sick when all these people are suffering!" Dr. Kasaria was shouting at Mordant, as John ducked back through the disinfectant field. "You're a terrible example of a Hyperspace High student. Wait until the headmaster hears about this."

"But I did feel awful, Dr. Kasaria," Mordant replied, holding up his hands. "It just seems to have passed now. What do you think it could have been?"

"Get out!" Dr. Kasaria barked. She glanced over her shoulder to see John standing where she had pushed him when Mordant "collapsed." "You, too, John. Get out of here now. I will be reporting you both for wasting my time during an emergency."

"Well?" Mordant Talliver asked as the two of them headed for the TravelTube. "Did you make sure everyone got a dose of gas? Did you see any improvement?"

"All of them got some," John replied, explaining how he had fed the gas into the oxygen system. "I don't know if it worked — but maybe . . ."

John remembered Kaal's long sigh as his convulsions stopped. He shrugged. "Too soon to tell, really."

"But you got everybody?" Mordant repeated, tugging at John's sleeve.

"I hope so," said John, shifting the remaining canisters in his arms. "Come on, there are the emergency wards to do yet."

"Okay," said Mordant, picking up his pace. "You distract the Meteor Medic this time; I'll let off the gas."

* * *

Once the canisters were empty, John and Mordant staggered back to the dormitories, exhausted almost beyond logic.

Pausing outside of his dorm room, John

looked at Mordant, who looked exhausted, and asked, "Now what?"

"Now we wait and see if it worked," Mordant said.

Shrugging, John said, "Well, goodnight, then." As Mordant turned to go, John added, "Hey, and thanks, Mordant."

Mordant nodded, then awkwardly raised a tentacle to give John a high five. "That's what you Earthlings do, right?"

With a weary grin, John touched Mordant's rubbery tentacle. Just then, a wailing siren sounded, and a green force field froze them both in place.

In their exhausted state, neither boy had noticed the Examiner who had floated in, until it suddenly droned, "MAJOR INFRACTION OF RULES NINE-FIFTY-SEVEN, THREE-EIGHTEEN B, THREE-FIVE-SIX,

AND TWO-TWO-FOUR SECTION C
DETECTED. PUNISHMENT: SOLITARY
CONFINEMENT."

CHAPTER 19

"John, for the third time, wake up and report immediately to the medical wing!" Zepp said urgently.

John stirred, turning around in surprise. He wasn't in his bed pod; he was lying on the hard floor of a cell, still wearing the flight suit from his trip to Zaleta Nebula.

Scrambling to sit upright, he shook his

head in confusion. Suddenly, the events of the previous night flooded back — he remembered that he and Mordant had been caught by the Examiner and locked in separate detention cells.

He rose to his feet stiffly and rubbed his eyes. "What's going on, Zepp? I'm in big trouble, right?"

Zepp turned the blaring alarm off and said, "Report immediately to the medical wing."

"Is it bad news?"

"I have been instructed not to give you any further information," Zepp replied. "I am sorry, John, but my orders came straight from the headmaster."

Oh no, this doesn't sound good at all, John thought nervously.

John shook his head in an attempt to clear the fuzz of sleep. He ran a hand through his hair, feeling how knotted and tangled it was.

"Has there been any improvement? Is Kaal still —"

"You are to report to medical wing immediately," Zepp repeated. "As in now."

"Okay," said John, rising to his feet. "I'm going."

Getting to the medical wing was like walking through a ghost ship. John didn't see a single being, not even a robot.

His heart sank. He guessed that hours had passed since he had released the nebula's microbes, but Hyperspace High was still deathly quiet.

He had hoped that by now everyone would be on the way to recovery.

It didn't work, he thought, reminding himself that no tests had ever been done on the microbes; it was only a hypothesis. Most scientists didn't believe there was a cure for Zhaldarian Flu.

Maybe the microbes aren't a cure at all. Maybe they just made everyone even sicker . . .

With that horrific thought, John picked up his pace and ran for the medical wing reception area.

Dr. Kasaria was waiting for him, her arms folded and a stern look on her face. She still wasn't looking very well, John noticed, but at least she was on her feet.

"I know you tricked me so that you could release that gas," she said, as he stepped through the doors.

John gulped. "I'm . . . ugh . . . sorry, D-Dr. Kasaria," he stammered. "The headmaster said that the microbes might —"

"Come with me, please. Quickly," the doctor said. She stepped briskly toward the door leading to the private wards.

"Is it Kaal?" babbled John, hurrying to keep

up. "Is he . . . ? I mean, he's still . . . um . . . he's alive, isn't he? The gas didn't make him worse?"

"See for yourself," said Dr. Kasaria, opening the door to Kaal's room.

For a moment, John felt as if the breath had been knocked out of him. His knees sagged. "Kaal?" he managed to croak.

"Hey," Kaal replied, raising his hand weakly in greeting.

John blinked. His friend was sitting up in bed. His skin was a strange shade of turquoise and it still sagged, but the fungus had gone and his eyes were open, full of life. As John struggled not to cry with relief, Kaal smiled, his sharp fangs clean and white.

"I hear you saved my life," Kaal rasped in a hoarse voice. "Thanks, John. I owe you one. Maybe I'll take it a little easier on you next time we play Boxogle." He even managed a weak smile.

On legs that felt like they were made of jelly, John crossed the floor to his friend's bedside. "You can repay me by getting better as fast as possible," he said, grinning. "I was totally bored without you around. There was no one to play virtual-reality games with."

John felt a hand on his shoulder and turned around to Dr. Kasaria's huge black eyes. They were sparkling with relief and joy.

"I'm sorry I didn't believe you, John," she said solemnly. "The headmaster arrived shortly after you left and told me what you had done. We watched over the patients through the night." Her voice became thick with emotion. "I've . . . I've never seen anything like it. It was incredible. I was sure I was going to start losing people last night, and instead everyone started getting better. I wanted to wake you up, so you could come and see what was happening, but the headmaster said you had earned your rest, and I know he was right."

"I would have liked to have been here," said John.

"Well, you're welcome to visit whenever you like," replied the doctor with a warm smile. "Though it looks as though every patient will be discharged soon. For now, there is someone else who would like to see you."

"Emmie!" John yelped, making for the door. He looked back over his shoulder. "Kaal, I'll see you in a while."

"You're not leaving me here," said Kaal. "Wait up, I'm coming with you."

John stopped, looking from Dr. Kasaria to

his friend and back again. "Are you sure that's a good idea?" he asked.

"It might be better if you stayed in bed," murmured the doctor.

"I've been in bed for days!" Kaal snorted, swinging his legs over the side of the bed and stretching out his wings. "And I can't imagine it's far, Dr. Kasaria."

The doctor smiled again. "I suppose there's no harm," she said.

Kaal was already crossing the room, pulling on a red and silver bathrobe.

A few seconds later, Kaal and John were leaning over Emmie's bed.

"Hi," John said gently, looking down into the Sillaran girl's navy blue eyes with a smile. "You're looking better than you were the last time I saw you."

Emmie tried to raise her head, but she was still too weak. With a sigh, she dropped back on the pillow. "Did I look as awful as I felt?" she whispered.

"You were kind of green," John said. "Not as bad as Kaal, though. He looked like he was turning into a mushroom."

Emmie's skin, he was pleased to see, had returned to its normal golden color. She was still pale, but it was obvious that her health was returning.

"How can I ever thank you, John?" she asked, reaching for his hand. "How can any of us ever thank you?"

John looked embarrassed. "It wasn't just me, you know," he said. "I had help."

"Who?" asked Kaal and Emmie at the same time.

"Mordant Talliver," replied John. Seeing the shock on his friends' faces, he continued quickly, "He was pretty cool, actually. No one else would come, but he volunteered and helped me get to the Zaleta Nebula."

"Wow, really?" Emmie said.

John nodded. Then he went on, "Then, when Dr. Kasaria wouldn't let us release the gas, he came up with this great plan to distract her. Without him, I would've failed. Plus, he saved me from getting hit by a meteor. I kind of owe him my life."

"You have got to be kidding me," said Kaal. "We're talking about the same Mordant Talliver, right? Black hair? Tentacles? Really bad attitude problem?"

John nodded. "Same Mordant Talliver," he said. "We broke about fifty school rules and . . .

oh shoot, I'd totally forgotten about that. I think we're going to be expelled."

"After you found a cure for Zhaldarian Flu and saved the lives of hundreds of people?" said Emmie, raising an eyebrow. "I don't think anyone's going to be expelling you."

"Maybe," said John. "Ah, I just remembered. I'm sorry, but I think I might have gotten your dad fired, too, Emmie."

"My dad?" squawked Emmie, this time managing to lift her head from the pillow. "How does my dad fit into all this?"

"Maybe I should start at the beginning," John said thoughtfully.

"Yes, maybe you should," Emmie replied.

* * *

Half an hour later, Emmie and Kaal were still asking questions.

"So you flew through an asteroid field in hyperspace?" Kaal said, shaking his head in disbelief. "That is the craziest thing I have ever heard. You could have been killed."

"What I still don't understand," Emmie cut in, "is why Mordant Talliver, of all people, offered to help." She paused for a moment, getting her breath back. "It doesn't sound like him at all."

"Maybe you should ask him," said Kaal, sitting up straighter and nodding toward the screen.

John and Emmie turned their heads to look. Mordant had arrived and was talking to Dr. Kasaria in the reception area. He had an anxious look on his face.

The doctor pointed through the screen toward the three friends.

A second later, Mordant Talliver stepped through the disinfectant field. With his gaze fixed on the other end of the ward, he walked straight past Emmie's bed, not even registering his classmates' presence. John saw silent tears rolling down the half-Gargon's cheeks as he rushed past.

Reaching Doctor Graal's bed, Mordant came to a halt — then collapsed to his knees.

For a moment, nothing happened. Then, Doctor Graal's black tentacles snaked out, wrapping him in a tight embrace.

"Oh, Mordant," said the Gargon teacher, her voice thick with emotion. "You brave, brave boy. Dr. Kasaria said you saved my life."

Mordant wrapped his arms and tentacles around her in return, sobbing openly now.

"You know I'd do anything for you, Mom," he croaked.

CHAPTER 20

"Hey, Riley!" shouted Lishtig, sprinting across the main hangar deck and weaving between milling students, with his long, purple ponytail streaming behind him. "John!"

"What?" John said, breaking off his conversation.

"I just saw what you and Talliver did to

Jegger's Talios 720," panted Lishtig, eyes wide. "It's a complete mess. Have you seen him yet?"

John shook his head.

"Well, I'd think seriously about moving to another galaxy if I were you," Lishtig said nervously. "He is totally going to beat you to death!"

"Thanks for reminding me, Lishtig," John said sarcastically. "I'm probably going to be paying for the damage to that ship for the rest of my life."

"You're welcome," replied Lishtig with a grin, ducking away and shouting, "Gobi! Gobi, where are you? You have to see this."

John sighed.

Sergeant Jegger was just one of the many things John now had to worry about. It had been three days since he had returned from the Zaleta

Nebula, and he still hadn't seen the headmaster. None of the Examiners had bothered him, but John was still unsure if he was in trouble for breaking so many school rules.

Not only that, but the exam results hadn't been posted, either. Every time John thought about the Hyperspace History exam, his stomach twisted.

What if they tell me I'm not coming back after the holidays? he thought. *Or even worse, what if I end up in, like, space prison for fifty years for breaking all those rules? I'll never see Emmie and Kaal again . . .*

"Enough frowning," Kaal said. The taller boy chuckled, punching John lightly on the arm. "Look around," he added, sweeping his wing in a half-circle. "You did this. You and Mordant Talliver, which — by the way — I still can't believe."

John looked around the main hangar deck, where gleaming silver shuttles were waiting to take students home for the holidays.

The hangar teemed with beings of every shape and size, from every corner of the universe. As he watched, a creature that looked like a large, leafless bush on rootlike legs ran past. A tiny girl with wings and four heads swooped after it, squeaking, "Come back here and say that to my faces, Frinnara!"

Here and there, a few students were leaning on their friends, still weak from their illness. But every single person who'd had the flu was on the way to a complete recovery.

"You worry about everything, strange Earthling," said Emmie. "Cheer up. Kaal's right, you saved hundreds of lives."

"Sorry," John said with a sheepish grin. "I

just can't help thinking what if I never see all this, and you guys, again."

"Well, I'm pretty sure I bombed on Cosmic Languages," Emmie said. "Apart from Space Flight, that was the only other exam I took, so if you failed, I failed, too."

"That's even worse," said John gloomily, sticking his hands in his pockets. "I mean, what if —"

"John!" both his friends shouted together.

He grinned. "Yeah, well, I suppose it could all turn out all right," he admitted. "And I am really looking forward to seeing my mom and —"

"Dad!" Emmie's scream interrupted him. Yelping with joy, she sprinted toward a TravelTube just as the door opened, revealing a tall, golden-skinned Sillaran with bluish-silver hair. He caught Emmie in his arms and hugged her as if he were going to squeeze the life out of her.

"Should we go and say hello?" asked Kaal, as Councillor Tarz put his daughter down, stared at her in delight, then picked her up and hugged her again.

"Good idea. I owe Emmie's dad a big thanks."

"Cadet Riley, wait right there!" barked Jegger's voice before John could even start walking.

"Oh no," John muttered to himself. He took a deep breath and turned to face the sergeant. *Here we go.*

"Sergeant Jegger," he said. "Before you say anything, can I just say how sorry I am about your Talios. If there's anything I can —"

"Save it, cadet," snapped Jegger. The flight instructor looked frail and was leaning heavily on a walking stick but, for the first time ever, John saw his teacher's face break into a wide smile.

Jegger clapped him on the shoulder. "I wanted to give you my thanks before you went off for the holidays. That was an amazing thing you did. Frankly, I think you deserve a medal. I'm proud of you, John Riley. We are all proud of you."

John stared into Jegger's face, unable to believe his ears. "But . . . but . . . there's so much damage," he managed to squawk.

"Oh well, the holidays get boring. Fixing it will keep me busy," replied Jegger, his gray mustache twitching with humor. "Done me a favor, really. I'm never happier than when

I'm tinkering around with her. And there was nothing left to do — so now I can start over again."

"Is this the famous John Riley?" boomed a voice that sounded vaguely familiar. It seemed to be coming from his knees.

Curiously, John looked down, into the smiling face of a tiny, wart-covered being with long, pointed ears.

"Sorry, I almost forgot," said Jegger, as John struggled to place the voice. "Cadet Riley, this is a former student of mine — Cadet . . . sorry . . . Captain Lassco."

That's where I've heard the voice before! John thought. He blinked. "Uh . . . Captain . . . nice to m-meet you," he stammered, not knowing quite what to say to the pilot who had tried to destroy him.

"I've been doing my research," said Captain Lassco, holding out a hand for John to take. "On your planet, this is how they say 'no hard feelings,' isn't it?"

"It is," replied John, reaching down to shake Captain Lassco's hand.

"That was quite an amazing chase," said Lassco. "There were a couple of moments I thought I was going to bite my own lips off . . . going through that asteroid field in hyperspace . . ." The little man shuddered, and then added, "Well, let's just say I won't be doing that again in a hurry."

"I didn't expect you to stay with me," John said with a smile.

"It was seriously impressive flying," replied Lassco. "Dangerous, but very impressive. If you ever want to join Starfighter Corps, let me know."

"Wow . . . that . . . that would be really cool."

"You've got a few more years training with me yet, cadet," Jegger cut in gruffly. "For now, I think Councillor Tarz is trying to get your attention."

"Thanks, Captain Lassco," John said, turning away. "Have a great holiday, Sergeant Jegger."

"Oh, I will," said Jegger, pulling a sonic hammer from his pocket and holding it up with a wink.

"I'm sorry — I can't keep quiet any longer," bellowed Emmie's father. His hand slapped John on the back, almost making his teeth rattle. "Good to see you again, son." His voice got serious. "I will never be able to express my gratitude to you, John."

John winced. "I'm just sorry you had to lose your job, sir," he said.

"Ha!" roared the tall Sillaran. "The president was furious. He called me every name in the galaxy and a few more I've never heard of. Sacked me on the spot and threatened to have me thrown in prison for treason."

"I'm so sorry," John choked out.

The councillor waved his hand. "Everything is fine," he said airily. "When it became obvious that you had saved the lives of the students and staff on board Hyperspace High and proved that a cure for Zhaldarian Flu exists, the president was forced to reinstate me." Peering down at John, he continued, "The Galactic Council and I are forever in your debt."

"I'm just glad Emmie and Kaal are better again," John said, blushing.

Councillor Tarz beamed at him. "Well, you know we already consider you part of the family.

Please let me know if there's ever anything I can do for you."

As the councillor gave Emmie one last hug and began walking away to his own ship, there was a flash of light as the headmaster materialized in front of the friends

"Kaal, Emmie," said Lorem, his purple eyes twinkling, "so good to see you looking like yourselves again."

John nodded in agreement, but couldn't bring himself to look Lorem in the eye.

"But you don't look very happy, John. What is troubling you?"

"It's, well . . . uh . . . all those rules I broke, sir," John mumbled.

Lorem raised an eyebrow. "One of the benefits of being the headmaster," he said with a chuckle, "is that I have access to the Examiners' central databank. The records of your . . . uh . . . adventures, have been wiped clean. Though the rest of us, of course, will never forget what we owe you."

Exhaling a huge sigh, John felt his shoulders drop with relief. But he quickly remembered that this wasn't the last of his problems. John took a deep breath and looked up into the headmaster's face.

"What about the exam results, sir?" John asked. "When do we all find out if we've passed?"

"In the circumstances, it would be unfair to judge any students by their exam results this term," Lorem replied. "They will not be entered on your records."

"You mean, we're all coming back next term?" gasped John.

"Oh, yes," replied the headmaster. "Definitely."

Kaal and Emmie beamed from ear to ear, and John knew that the grin on his own face was just as wide.

"If you'll excuse us," Lorem said to Kaal and Emmie, "I'd like a word with John and Mordant in private. I won't keep them long."

John nodded a greeting to Mordant Talliver as the headmaster beckoned him over. But the half-Gargon boy made no sign that he had noticed.

At his shoulder, G-Vez drawled, "Keep your distance from young Master Talliver, Earthling. He does not wish to —"

"Shut up, G-Vez, or I'll melt you down for scrap," ordered Mordant, stopping beside John and returning the nod at last.

Lorem looked first into John's face and then into Mordant's. "I wanted to add my own thanks to those of everyone else on the ship," he said gravely. "Because of your bravery, everyone has survived. I know that neither of you finds it easy to get along, but I hope that you'll take some time to reflect on what might have happened if you had not worked together."

The two boys glanced at each other.

"In the meantime," the headmaster went on, "I am enormously proud of you both. Thank you again, and I look forward to seeing you both back here next term."

"Zepp deserves some thanks, too, sir," said John. "We would never have been able to leave the ship if it weren't for him doing me a favor. Plus, the Examiners would still have us in a detention room."

"You're welcome, friend," said Zepp's voice.

"Now you'll have to excuse me, I have a few more goodbyes to say," said Lorem, disappearing in a flash of light.

"Mordant!" called Doctor Graal. "Come and say goodbye before you go to your father's."

"Just a minute, Mom!" Mordant shouted over his shoulder.

Turning back to John, he put out a tentacle. "Who knows. Maybe he's right," he said, tilting his head toward the headmaster, who was now laughing in the middle of another group of students.

"What — about it not being easy working together?"

A smile flickered across Mordant's face. "No, about what might have happened if we hadn't, idiot."

John took hold of Mordant's tentacle and shook it. "Why didn't you tell anyone Doctor Graal was your mother?" he asked.

Mordant shrugged. "Didn't want everyone thinking I was best in the class just because my mom's the teacher," he said.

At that moment, Doctor Graal appeared beside him.

"Come on, darling boy. You can't keep me waiting all day," she slobbered, wrapping her tentacles around her son and pulling him into a hug.

"Aww, Mom, stop it," Mordant said. "You're embarrassing me."

"Um . . . John, Ms. Vartexia's trying to get everyone onboard shuttle thirty-six," Kaal said. He appeared with Emmie at his side and nudged John. "That's us."

"You know what she's like," said Emmie. "She's already got her ThinScreen out, making notes on anyone who's late."

A few seconds later, John bounded up the steps into the shuttle, falling into a seat between his friends. Something hit him on the head as his safety harness fastened around him.

"Have a Dumpod Candy, John!" shouted Lishtig.

"There will be no food fights aboard this shuttle," announced Ms. Vartexia sternly, climbing the steps. "No food fights, no Bubble Bombs, no Shuttle Surfing, no . . ."

Her voice was drowned out by loud groans from all the students.

"All shuttles," said Zepp's voice loudly, "prepare for departure."

John felt a tremor run through the shuttle

as the engines started. Ahead, the massive bay doors opened out to space.

"So, good term?"

John turned to see Kaal grinning at him.

"Not bad," replied Emmie from John's other side. "But I thought there was too much Hyperspace History, Galactic Geography, Cosmic Languages, and well . . . you get the idea."

Laughing, John said, "So, you didn't mind almost getting blown up on Zirion Beta, fighting Subo warriors —"

Emmie's nose wrinkled. "I would much rather get blown up and fight a Subo than have double Cosmic Languages," she claimed, her face deadly serious. "Hey, how about you, Kaal?"

"It was pretty exciting," said Kaal. "But I'm

looking forward to a nice quiet term when we get back."

"Shuttle thirty-six launch," said Zepp.

When we get back, John thought, as the shuttle slammed into space. While G-force pushed him back in his seat, a smile spread across John's face. For the past few days, he hadn't dared hope that he might be returning to Hyperspace High.

Glancing over his shoulder, he watched as its vast, elegant white shape disappeared behind him. He was already bursting with excitement at the thought of seeing his parents after a whole term away, but the holidays would be even better knowing that he would be returning to Hyperspace High after all.

His thoughts were interrupted by a shout from the row behind.

Lishtig was floating down the shuttle's cabin.

"Zero-G war!" the purple-haired boy bellowed.

"Lishtig ar Steero," snapped Ms. Vartexia. "I said —"

"You didn't say no Zero-G war," said Lishtig, sounding disappointed. "Please, Ms. Vartexia. Shuttle flights are so boring. Just for a few minutes."

The Elvian teacher sighed, and then surrendered. "All right, five minutes of Zero-G war. I will read my ThinScreen quietly and pretend I can't hear you."

John was already unclipping his harness. As his body floated above his seat, a huge grin spread across his face.

This really is the best school in the universe!

HYPERSPACE HIGH

READ THEM ALL!